Have you got all
FAMOUS F......

(*Also available as dramatised recordings on CD)

# A Note from Enid Blyton's Granddaughter

Welcome to the new edition of The Famous Five series by Enid Blyton. There are 21 books in the collection, a whole world of mystery and adventure to explore. My grandmother, Enid Blyton, wrote her first Famous Five Book, 'Five on a Treasure Island' in 1942. That was in the middle of World War Two (1939–1945). In the story, Julian, Dick and Anne meet their cousin Georgina and her dog, Timmy, for the first time. They soon learn *never* to call her Georgina. Together they explore tunnels and caves, discover hidden passageways and solve crimes.

I first met the Famous Five in a recording of 'Five have a Mystery to Solve'. Julian, Dick, George, Anne and Timmy have developed a love of sausages and can't seem to get enough of them. The sausages are put on hold when a lady knocks at the door of Kirrin Cottage. She has come to ask if the Five could keep her young grandson company in a remote cottage while she is away. The adventure begins as soon as they see the mysterious 'Whispering Island' as they cycle to the cottage to meet the grandson, Wilfred.

Timmy has always been my favourite character. He is the best judge of personality and when he is around, everything seems much safer; not that I am scared of adventure! Since watching the Famous Five television series in the 1970s, which cast Timmy as a Border-Collie sheep dog, I have always wanted to have a Border-Collie.

Who do you think you'll like best?

*Sophie Smallwood, 14 June 2010*

# Five Run
# Away Together

# Enid Blyton

# THE FAMOUS FIVE

## Five Run Away Together

Hodder
Children's
Books

A division of Hachette Children's Books

First published in Great Britain in 1944 by Hodder and Stoughton

This revised edition first published in 2010 by Hodder Children's Books

With thanks to Rachel Elliot

4

A Catalogue record for this book is available from the British Library

ISBN 978 0 340 93161 5

Typeset by Avon DataSet Ltd, Bidford-on-Avon, Warwickshire

Printed and bound in Great Britain by Clays Ltd, St Ives plc

The paper and board used in this paperback by Hodder Children's Books
are natural recyclable products made from wood grown in sustainable
forests. The manufacturing processes conform to the environmental
regulations of the country of origin.

Hodder Children's Books
a division of Hachette Children's Books
338 Euston Road, London NW1 3BH
An Hachette UK company
www.hachette.co.uk

# *Contents*

20  The thieves – and a new prisoner
21  A visit to the police station
22  Back to Kirrin Island!

# 1  Summer holidays

'George, please settle down and do something,' said George's mother. 'You keep wandering in and out with Timothy, and I'm trying to have a rest.'

'Sorry, Mum,' said Georgina, taking hold of Timothy's collar. 'But I feel lonely without the others. I wish tomorrow would come. I've been without them for three whole weeks already.'

Georgina went to boarding school with her cousin Anne, and in the holidays she and Anne, and Anne's two brothers, Julian and Dick, usually joined up together and had plenty of fun. Now it was the summer holidays, and already three weeks had gone by. Anne, Dick and Julian had gone away with their father and mother, but Georgina's parents had wanted her with them, so she had not gone.

Now her three cousins were coming the next day to spend the rest of the summer holidays with her at her old home, Kirrin Cottage.

'It will be lovely when they are here,' said George, as she was always called, to Timothy her dog. 'Absolutely lovely, Timothy. Don't you think so?'

'Woof,' said Timothy and licked George's hand.

George was dressed, as usual, exactly like a boy, in jeans and a jumper. She had always wanted to be a boy, and would never answer if she was called Georgina. So everyone called her George. She had missed her cousins very much during the first weeks of the summer holidays.

'I used to think I liked best to be alone,' George said to Timothy, who always seemed to understand every word she said. 'But now I know that was silly. It's nice to be with others and share things, and make friends.'

Timothy thumped his tail on the ground. He certainly liked being with the others too. He was longing to see Julian, Anne and Dick again.

George took Timothy down to the beach. She shaded her eyes with her hand, and looked out to the entrance of the bay. In the middle of it, almost as if it were guarding it, lay a small, rocky island, on which rose the ruins of an old castle.

'We'll visit you again this summer, Kirrin Island,' said George softly. 'I haven't been able to go to you yet this summer, because my boat was being mended – but it will be ready soon, then I'll come to you. And I'll look all around the old castle again. Oh Tim – do you remember the adventures we had on Kirrin Island last summer?'

Tim remembered quite well, because he had shared in the thrilling adventures. He had been down in the dungeons of the castle with the others; he had helped to find treasure there, and had had just as exciting a time as the four children he loved. He gave a little bark.

'You're remembering, aren't you, Tim?' said George, patting him. 'Won't it be fun to go there again? We'll go down into the dungeons again, shall we? Do you remember how Dick climbed down the deep well-shaft to rescue us?'

It was exciting, remembering all the things that had happened last year. It made George long all the more for the next day, when her three friends would arrive.

'I wish Mum would let us go and live on the island for a week,' thought George. 'That would be amazing fun – to live on my very own island!'

It was George's island. It really belonged to her

mother, but she had said, two or three years back, that George could have it, and George now thought of it as really her own. She felt that all the rabbits on it belonged to her, all the wild birds and other creatures.

'I'll suggest that we go there for a week, when the others come,' she thought, excitedly. 'We'll take our food and everything, and live there completely by ourselves. We'll feel like Robinson Crusoe.'

She went to meet her cousins the next day, driving the pony and trap by herself. Her mother wanted to come, but she said she didn't feel very well. George felt a bit worried about her. So often lately her mother had said she didn't feel very well. Perhaps it was the heat of the summer. The weather had been very hot lately. Day after day had brought nothing but blue sky and sunshine. George had a healthy brown glow, and her eyes looked startlingly blue against her face. She had had her hair cut even shorter than usual, and it really was difficult to know whether she was a boy or a girl.

The train came in. Three hands waved madly from a window, and George shouted in delight.

'Julian! Dick! Anne! You're here at last.'

The three children tumbled out of their carriage. Julian yelled to a porter.

'Our bags are in the guard's van. Hello, George! How are you? You've grown!'

They all had. They were all a year older and a year bigger than when they had had their exciting adventures on Kirrin Island. Even Anne, the youngest, didn't look so small now. She flung herself on George, almost knocking her over, and then went down on her knees beside Timothy, who was quite mad with joy to see his three friends.

There was a terrific noise. They all shouted their news at once, and Timothy barked without stopping.

'We thought the train would never get here!'

'Oh Timothy, you darling, you're just the same as ever!'

'Woof, woof, woof!'

'Mother's sorry she couldn't come and meet you too.'

'George, how well you look! Aren't we going to have fun!'

'WOOF, WOOF!'

'Shut up, Tim, and get down; you've bitten my tie almost in half. Oh, you dear old dog, it's great to see you!'.

'Woof!'

The porter wheeled up their luggage, and soon it was in the pony cart. George clicked to the waiting pony, and it cantered off. The five in the little cart all talked at once at the top of their voices, Tim far more loudly than anyone else, for his doggy voice was strong and powerful.

'I hope your mother isn't ill?' said Julian, who was fond of his aunt. She was gentle and kind, and loved having them all.

'I think it must be the heat,' said George.

'What about Uncle Quentin?' asked Anne. 'Is he all right?'

The three children didn't like George's father very much. He could be very grumpy, and although he welcomed the three cousins to his house, he didn't really like children. So they always felt a little awkward with him, and were glad when he wasn't there.

'Dad's all right,' said George, cheerfully. 'Only he's worried about Mum. He doesn't seem to notice her much when she's well and cheerful, but he gets awfully upset if anything goes wrong with her. So be a bit careful of him at the moment. You know what he's like when he's worried.'

The children did know. Uncle Quentin was best avoided when things went wrong. But not even the thought of a cross uncle could depress them today. They were on holiday; they were going to Kirrin Cottage; they were by the sea, and there was dear old Timothy beside them, and fun of all kinds in store.

'Shall we go to Kirrin Island, George?' asked Anne. 'We haven't been there since last summer. The weather was too bad in the winter and Easter holidays. Now it's gorgeous.'

'Of course we'll go,' said George, her blue eyes shining. 'Do you know what I thought? I thought it would be brilliant to go and stay there for a whole week by ourselves! We're older now, and I'm sure Mum would let us.'

'Go and stay on your island for a week!' cried Anne. 'Oh! That would be too good to be true.'

'*Our* island,' said George, happily. 'Don't you remember I said I'd divide it into four, and we'd all share it? Well, I meant it, you know. It's ours, not mine.'

'What about Timothy?' said Anne. 'Shouldn't he have a share as well? Can't we make it five bits, one for him too?'

'He can share mine,' said George. She drew the pony to a stop, and the four children and the dog gazed out across the blue bay. 'There's Kirrin Island,' said George. 'I can hardly wait to get to it now. I haven't been able to go there yet, because my boat wasn't mended.'

'Then we can all go together,' said Dick. 'I wonder if the rabbits are just as tame as ever.'

'Woof!' said Timothy at once. He had only to hear the word 'rabbits' to get excited.

'It's no good thinking about the rabbits on Kirrin,' said George. 'You know I don't allow you to chase them, Tim.'

Timothy's tail dropped and he looked mournfully at George. It was the only thing on which he and George didn't agree. Tim was firmly convinced that rabbits were meant for him to chase, and George was just as firmly convinced that they weren't.

'Get on!' said George to the pony, and jerked the reins. The little creature trotted on towards Kirrin Cottage, and very soon they were all opposite the front gate.

A sour-faced woman came out from the back door to help them down with their luggage. The children didn't know her.

'Who's she?' they whispered to George.

'The new cook,' said George. 'Joanna had to go and look after her mother, who broke her leg. Then Mother got this cook – her name's Mrs Stick.'

'Good name for her,' grinned Julian. 'She looks a real old stick! But I hope she doesn't stick here for long. I hope Joanna comes back. I liked old Joanna, and she was nice to Timmy.'

'Mrs Stick has a dog too,' said George. 'A horrible animal, smaller than Tim, all sort of mangy and moth-eaten. Tim can't bear it.'

'Where is it?' asked Anne, looking around.

'It's kept in the kitchen, and Tim isn't allowed near it,' said George. 'Good thing too, because I'm sure he'd eat it! He can't think what's in the kitchen, and goes sniffing around the shut door till Mrs Stick nearly goes mad.'

The others laughed. They had all climbed down from the pony cart now, and were ready to go indoors. Julian helped Mrs Stick in with all the bags. George took the pony cart away, and the other three went in to say hello to their uncle and aunt.

'Well, hello!' said Aunt Fanny, smiling at them from the sofa where she was lying down. 'How are you all? I'm sorry I couldn't come to meet you. Uncle Quentin is out for a walk. You had better go upstairs, and wash and change. Then come down for tea.'

The boys went up to their old bedroom, with its funny slanting roof, and its window looking out over the bay. Anne went to the little room she shared with George. How good it was to be back again at Kirrin! What fun they would have these holidays with George and Timmy!

## 2 The Stick family

It was lovely to wake up the next morning at Kirrin Cottage and see the sun shining in at the windows, and to hear the far-off plash-plash-plash of the sea. It was wonderful to leap out of bed and rush to see how blue the sea was, and how lovely Kirrin Island looked at the entrance of the bay.

'I'm going for a swim before breakfast,' said Julian, grabbing his trunks. 'Coming, Dick?'

'Definitely!' said Dick. 'Call the girls. We'll all go.'

So down they went, the four of them, with Tim galloping behind them, his tail wagging nineteen to the dozen, and his long pink tongue hanging out of his mouth. He went into the water with the others, and swam all around them. They were all good swimmers, but Julian and George were the best.

They put towels around themselves, rubbed

their bodies dry and pulled on jeans and jumpers.
Then back to breakfast they went, as hungry as
hunters. Anne noticed a boy in the back garden
and stared in surprise.

'Who's that?' she said.

'Oh, that's Edgar, Mrs Stick's boy,' said George.
'I don't like him. He's always sticking out his
tongue and shouting rude words.'

Edgar was singing when the others went in at
the gate. Anne stopped to listen.

'Georgie-porgie, pudding and pie!' sang Edgar,
a silly look on his face. He seemed about thirteen
or fourteen, a stupid, yet sly-looking lad. 'Georgie-
porgie pudding and pie!'

George went red.

'He's always singing that,' she said, furiously.
'Just because I'm called "George", I suppose. He
thinks he's clever. I can't stand him.'

Julian called out to Edgar. 'You shut up! You're
not funny, you're just silly!'

'Georgie-porgie,' began Edgar again, a silly
smile on his wide red face.

Julian made a step towards him, and he at once
disappeared into the house.

'I can't stand much of *him*,' said Julian, in a

decided voice. 'I'm amazed *you* do, George. It's a wonder you haven't slapped his face, stamped on his foot, bitten his ears off and done a few other things! You used to be so fierce.'

'Well – I am still, really,' said George. 'I *feel* fierce down inside me when I hear Edgar singing silly songs at me like that and calling me names – but you see, Mum really hasn't been well, and I know if I go for Edgar, Mrs Stick will leave, and poor Mum would have to do all the housework, and she really isn't fit to at present. So I just hold myself in, and hope that Timmy will do the same.'

'Good for *you*,' said Julian, admiringly, for he knew how hard it was for George to keep her temper at times.

'I think I'll just go up to Mum's room and see if she'd like breakfast in bed,' said George. 'Hang on to Timmy a moment, will you? If Edgar turns up again, he might go for him.'

Julian hung on to Timmy's collar. Timmy had growled when Edgar had been in the garden. Now he stood stock still, his nose twitching as if he were trying to trace a smell.

Suddenly a mangy-looking dog appeared out

of the kitchen door. It had a dirty white coat, out of which patches seemed to have been bitten, and its tail was well between its legs.

'Wooooof!' said Timmy, joyfully, and leapt at the dog. He pulled Julian over, for he was a big dog, and the boy let go of the dog's collar. Timmy pounced excitedly on the other dog, who gave a scared whine and tried to go into the kitchen again.

'Timmy! Come here!' yelled Julian. But Timmy didn't hear. He was busy trying to snap off the other dog's ears – or at least, that's what he appeared to be doing. The other dog yelped for help, and Mrs Stick appeared at the kitchen door, a saucepan in her hand.

'Call off that dog!' she screeched. She hit out at Timmy with the saucepan, but he dodged and it hit her own dog instead, making it yelp all the more.

'Don't hit out with that!' said Julian. 'You'll hurt the dogs. Timmy, TIMMY!'

Edgar now appeared, looking very scared. He picked up a stone and seemed to be about to hurl it at Timmy. Anne shrieked.

'You're not to throw that stone; you're not

to! You wicked, horrible boy!'

In the middle of all this turmoil Uncle Quentin appeared, looking angry and irritable.

'What is going on? I never heard such a racket in my life.'

Then George appeared, flying out of the door like the wind to rescue her beloved Timothy. She rushed to the two dogs and tried to pull Timmy away. Her father yelled at her.

'Come away, you silly child! Don't you know better than to separate two fighting dogs with your bare hands? Where's the garden hose?'

It was fixed to a tap nearby. Julian ran to it and turned on the tap. He picked up the hose and turned it on the two dogs. At once the jet of water spurted out at them, and they leapt apart in surprise. Julian saw Edgar standing near, and couldn't resist swinging the hose a little so that the boy was soaked. He gave a scream and ran in at once.

'What did you do that for?' said Uncle Quentin, annoyed. 'George, tie Timothy up at once. Mrs Stick, didn't I tell you not to let your dog out of the kitchen unless you had him on a lead? I won't have this kind of thing happening. Where's breakfast? Late as usual!'

Mrs Stick disappeared into the kitchen, muttering and grumbling, taking her drenched dog with her. George, looking sulky, tied Timothy up. He lay down in his kennel, looking pleadingly up at her.

'I've told you not to take any notice of that mangy-looking dog,' said George, severely. 'Now you see what happens! You put Dad into a bad temper for the rest of the day, and Mrs Stick will be so angry she won't make any cakes for tea!'

Timmy gave a whine, and put his head down on his paws. He licked a few hairs from the corner of his mouth. It was sad to be tied up – but at least he had bitten a bit off the tip of one of that horrible dog's ears!

They all went in to breakfast. 'Sorry I let Timmy go,' said Julian to George. 'But he nearly tore my arm off. I couldn't hold him! He's grown into a really powerful dog, hasn't he?'

'Yes,' said George, proudly. 'He has. He could eat Mrs Stick's dog up in a mouthful if we'd let him. And Edgar too.'

'And Mrs Stick,' said Anne. 'All of them. I don't like any of them.'

Breakfast was rather a subdued meal, as Aunt Fanny wasn't there, but Uncle Quentin was – and Uncle Quentin in a bad temper wasn't a very cheerful person to have at the breakfast table. He snapped at George and glared at the others. Anne almost wished they hadn't come to Kirrin Cottage! But she felt better when she thought of the rest of the day – they would take their dinner out, perhaps, and have it on the beach – or maybe even go out to Kirrin Island. Uncle Quentin wouldn't be with them to spoil things.

Mrs Stick came to clear away the porridge plates and bring in the bacon. She banged the plates down on the table.

'No need to do that,' said Uncle Quentin, irritably. Mrs Stick said nothing. She was scared of Uncle Quentin, and no wonder! She put the next lot of plates down quietly.

'What are you going to do today?' asked Uncle Quentin, towards the end of breakfast. He was feeling a bit better, and didn't like to see such subdued faces around him.

'We thought we might go out for a picnic,' said George, eagerly. 'I asked Mum. She said we can, if Mrs Stick will make us sandwiches.'

'Well, I shouldn't think she'll try very hard,' said Uncle Quentin, trying to make a little joke. They all smiled politely. 'But you can ask her.'

There was a silence. Nobody liked the idea of asking Mrs Stick for sandwiches.

'I wish she hadn't brought Stinker,' said George, gloomily. 'Everything would be easier if he wasn't here.'

'Is that the name of her son?' asked Uncle Quentin in surprise.

George grinned. 'No. Although it wouldn't be a bad name for him, because he hardly ever has a bath, and he's really smelly. It's her dog I mean. She calls him Tinker, but I call him Stinker because he smells so awful.'

'I don't think that's a very nice name,' said her father, in the midst of the others' giggles.

'No, it isn't,' said George, 'but then, he isn't a very nice dog.'

In the end it was Aunt Fanny who saw Mrs Stick and arranged about the sandwiches. Mrs Stick went up to see Aunt Fanny, who was having breakfast in bed, and agreed to make sandwiches, though with a very bad grace.

'I didn't bargain for three more children to come traipsing along,' she said, sulkily.

'I told you they were coming, Mrs Stick,' said Aunt Fanny, patiently. 'I didn't know I would be feeling so ill myself when they came. If I had been well I could have made their sandwiches and done many more things. I can only ask you to help as much as you can till I feel better. I may be all right tomorrow. Let the children have a good time for a week or so, and then, if I still feel ill, I'm sure they will all turn to and help a bit. But let them have a good time first.'

The children took their packets of sandwiches and set off. On the way they met Edgar, looking as stupid and sly as usual.

'Why don't you let me come along with you?' he said. 'Let's go to that island. I know a lot about it.'

'No, you don't,' said George, in a flash. 'You don't know anything about it. And I'd never take *you*. It's *my* island. Well, *ours*. It belongs to all four of us and Timmy, too. We'd never allow you to go.'

''Tisn't your island,' said Edgar. 'That's a lie, that is!'

'You don't know what you're talking about,' said George, scornfully. 'Come on, you lot! We can't waste time talking to Edgar.'

They left him looking sulky and angry. As soon as they were at a safe distance he lifted up his voice:

> '*Georgie-porgie, pudding and pie,*
> *She knows how to tell a lie,*
> *Georgie-porgie, pudding and pie!*'

Julian started to go back after him, but George pulled him on.

'He'll only go and tell tales to his mother, and she'll walk out and there'll be no one to help Mum,' she said. 'I'll just have to put up with it. Let's try and think of some way to get our own back, though. I can't stand him! I hate his pimply nose and screwed-up eyes.'

'Woof!' said Timmy, feelingly.

'Timmy says he hates Stinker's miserable tail and silly little ears,' explained George, and they all laughed. That made them feel better. They were soon out of hearing of Edgar's silly song, and forgot all about him.

'Let's go and see if your boat is ready,' said Julian. 'Then maybe we could row out to the island.'

## 3 A nasty shock

George's boat was almost ready, but not quite. It was having a last coat of paint on it. It looked very nice, for George had chosen a bright red paint, and the oars were painted red too.

'Oh, can't we possibly have it this afternoon?' said George to Jim the boatman.

He shook his head.

'No, George,' he said, 'not unless you all want to be messed up with red paint. It'll be dry tomorrow, but not before.'

'We'll go to the island tomorrow then,' said Julian. 'We'll just picnic on the beach today. Then we'll go for a walk.'

So they picnicked on the sands with Timothy sharing more than half their lunch. The sandwiches weren't very nice. The bread was too stale; there wasn't enough butter inside, and they were far too thick. But Timothy didn't mind. He gobbled up as many as he could, his tail wagging so hard that it sent sand over everyone.

'Timothy, please take your tail out of the sand if you want to wag it,' said Julian, getting sand all over his hair for the fourth time. Timmy wagged his tail hard again, and sent another shower over Julian. Everyone laughed.

'Let's go for a walk now,' said Dick, jumping up. 'My legs could do with some good exercise. Where shall we go?'

'We'll walk along the cliff-top, where we can see the island all the time, shall we?' said Anne. 'George, is the old wreck still there?'

George nodded. The children had once had a very exciting time with an old wreck that had lain at the bottom of the sea. A great storm had lifted it up and set it firmly on the rocks. They had been able to explore the wreck then, and had found a map of the castle in it, with instructions as to where hidden treasure was to be found.

'Do you remember how we found that old map in the wreck, and how we looked for the ingots of gold and found them?' said Julian, his eyes gleaming as he remembered it all. 'Isn't the wreck battered to pieces yet, George?'

'No,' said George. 'I don't think so. It's on

the rocks on the other side of the island, you remember, so we can't see it from here. But we could have a look at it when we go on the island tomorrow.'

'Yes, let's,' said Anne. 'Poor old wreck! I guess it won't last many winters now.'

They walked along the cliff-top with Timothy capering ahead of them. They could see the island easily and the ruined castle rising up from the middle.

'There's the jackdaw tower,' said Anne, looking. 'The other tower's fallen down, hasn't it? Look at the jackdaws circling round and round the tower, George!'

'Yes. They build in it every year,' said George. 'Don't you remember the masses of sticks around the tower that the jackdaws dropped when they built their nests? We picked some up and made a fire with them once.'

'I'd love to do that again,' said Anne. 'Let's do it each night if we stay a week on the island. George, did you ask your mum?'

'Oh yes,' said George. 'She said she thought we might, but she would see.'

'I don't like it when grown-ups say they'll see,'

said Anne. 'It so often means they won't let you do something after all, but they don't like to tell you at the time.'

'Well, I expect she will let us,' said George. 'After all, we're much older than last year. Julian's in his teens already, and I soon shall be and so will Dick. Only Anne is small.'

'I'm not,' said Anne, indignantly. 'I'm as strong as you are. I can't help being younger.'

'There, there, baby!' said Julian, patting his little sister on the back and laughing at her furious face. 'Oh look! What's that over there on the island?'

He had caught sight of something as he was teasing Anne. Everyone swung around and gazed at Kirrin. George gave an exclamation.

'Look – a spire of smoke! Surely it's smoke? Someone's on my island.'

'On *our* island,' corrected Dick. 'It can't be! That smoke must come from one of those steamships out beyond the island. We can't see it, that's all. But I bet the smoke comes from a steamer. We know no one can get to the island except us. They don't know the way.'

'If anyone's on my island,' began George,

looking very fierce and angry, 'if anyone's on my island, I'll – I'll – I'll . . .'

'You'll explode and go up in smoke!' said Dick. 'There – it's gone now. I'm sure it was only a steamer letting off steam or smoking hard, whatever they do.'

They watched Kirrin Island for some time after that, but they could see no more smoke. 'If only my boat was ready!' said George, restlessly. 'I'd go over this afternoon. I've a good mind to go and get my boat, even if the paint *is* wet.'

'Don't be an idiot!' said Julian. 'You know what trouble we'd get into if we go home with all our things bright red. Have a bit of sense, George.'

George gave up the idea. She watched for a steamer to appear at one side of the island or another, to come into the bay, but none came.

'Probably anchored out there,' said Dick. 'Come on! Are we going to stand rooted to this spot for the rest of the day?'

'We'd better get back home,' said Julian, looking at his watch. 'It's almost tea-time. I hope your mum is up, George. It's much nicer when she's at meals.'

'Oh, I expect she will be,' said George. 'Come on then, let's go back!'

They turned to go back. They watched Kirrin Island as they walked, but all they could see were jackdaws or gulls in the sky above it. No more spires of smoke appeared. It must have been a steamer!

'All the same, I'm going over tomorrow to have a look,' said George, firmly. 'If any tourists are visiting my island I'll turn them off.'

'*Our* island,' said Dick. 'George, I wish you'd remember you said you'd share it with us.'

'Well – I did share it with you,' said George, 'but I can't help feeling it's still my island. Come on! I'm getting hungry.'

They came back at last to Kirrin Cottage. They went into the hall, and then into the sitting room. To their great surprise Edgar was there, reading one of Julian's books.

'What are you doing here?' said Julian. 'And who said you could borrow my book?'

'I'm not doing any harm,' said Edgar. 'If I want to have a quiet read, why shouldn't I?'

'You wait till my dad comes in and finds you lolling about here,' said George. 'If you'd gone into his study, you'd have been sorry.'

'I've been in there,' said Edgar, surprisingly. 'I've seen those funny instruments he's working with.'

'How *dare* you!' said George, going white with rage. 'Even *we* are not allowed to go into my dad's study. As for touching his things – well!'

Julian eyed Edgar curiously. He couldn't imagine why the boy should suddenly be so cheeky.

'Where's your father, George?' he said. 'I think we had better get him to deal with Edgar. He must be mad.'

'Call him if you like,' said Edgar, still lolling in the chair, and flicking through the pages of Julian's book in a very irritating way. 'He won't come.'

'What do you mean?' said George, feeling suddenly scared. 'Where's my mum?'

'Call her too, if you like,' said the boy, looking sly. 'Go on! Call her.'

The children suddenly felt afraid. What did Edgar mean? George flew upstairs to her mother's room, shouting loudly.

'Mum! Mum! Where are you?'

But her mother's bed was empty. It had not been made – but it was empty. George flew into all the other bedrooms, shouting desperately: 'Mum! Mum! Dad! Where are you?'

But there was no answer. George ran downstairs, her face very white. Edgar grinned up at her.

'What did I tell you?' he said. 'I said you could call all you liked, but they wouldn't come.'

'Where are they?' demanded George. 'Tell me at once!'

'Find out yourself,' said Edgar.

There was a resounding slap, and Edgar leapt to his feet, holding his left cheek with his hand. George had flown at him and dealt him the hardest smack she could. Edgar lifted his hand to slap her back, but Julian stood in front.

'You're not fighting George,' he said. 'If you want a fight, I'll take you on.'

'I'll fight Edgar, and I'll beat him, you see if I don't,' shouted George, trying to push Julian away.

But Julian kept her off. Edgar began to edge towards the doorway, but he found Dick there.

'One minute,' said Dick. 'Before you go – where are our uncle and aunt?'

'Gr-r-r-r-r-r,' suddenly said Timothy, in such a threatening voice that Edgar stared at him in fright. The dog had bared his great teeth, and had put up the hackles on his neck. He looked very frightening.

'Hold that dog!' said Edgar, his voice trembling. 'He looks as if he's going to jump at me.'

Julian put his hand on Tim's collar. 'Quiet, Tim!' he said. 'Now, Edgar, tell us what we want to know, and tell us quickly, or you'll be sorry.'

'Well, there isn't much to tell,' said Edgar, keeping his eye on Timothy. He shot a look at George and went on. 'Your mum was suddenly taken very ill – with a terrible pain *here* – and they got the doctor and they've taken her away to hospital, and your dad went with her. That's all!'

George sat down on the sofa, looking paler still and rather sick.

'Oh!' she said. 'Poor Mum! I wish I hadn't gone out today. How can we find out what's happened?'

Edgar had slipped out of the room, shutting the door behind him so that Timmy should not follow. The kitchen door was slammed, too. The children stared at one another, feeling upset and worried. Poor George! Poor Aunt Fanny!

'There must be a note somewhere,' said Julian, and looked around the room. He saw a letter stuck into the rim of the big mirror there, addressed to George. He gave it to her. It was from George's father.

'Read it, quickly,' said Anne. 'Oh dear – what a horrible start to our holiday!'

## 4 A few little upsets

George read the letter out loud. It wasn't very long, and had evidently been written in a great hurry.

DEAR GEORGE,

Your mother has been taken very ill. I'm going with her to the hospital. I won't leave her till she's getting better. That may be in a few days' time, or in a week's time. I'll telephone you each day at nine o'clock in the morning to tell you how she is. Mrs Stick will look after you all. Try to manage all right till I come back.

Your loving

FATHER

'Oh dear!' said Anne, knowing how dreadful George must feel. George loved her mother dearly, and for once the girl had tears in her eyes. George never cried – but it was terrible to come home and find her mother gone like this. And her father too! No one there but Mrs Stick and Edgar.

'I can't bear Mum going like this,' sobbed George, suddenly, and buried her head in a cushion. 'She – she might never come back.'

'Don't be silly, George,' said Julian, sitting down and putting his arm around her. 'Of course she will. Why shouldn't she? Didn't your father say he was staying with her till she was getting better – and that would be probably in a few days' time. Cheer up, George! It isn't like you to give way like this.'

'But I didn't say goodbye,' sobbed poor George. 'And I made her ask Mrs Stick for the sandwiches, instead of me. I want to go and find Mum and see how she is myself.'

'You don't know where they've taken her, and if you did, they wouldn't let you in,' said Dick, gently. 'Let's have some tea. We'll all feel better after that.'

'I couldn't eat *any*thing,' said George, fiercely. Timothy pushed his nose into her hands, and tried to lick them. They were under her buried face. The dog whined a little.

'Poor Timmy! He can't understand,' said Anne. 'He's upset because you're unhappy, George.'

That made George sit up. She rubbed her hands over her eyes, and let Timmy lick the wet tears off them. He looked surprised at the salty taste. He tried to get on to George's knee.

'Silly Timmy!' said George, in a more ordinary voice. 'Don't be upset. I just got a shock, that's all! I'm better now, Timmy. Don't whine like that, silly! I'm all right. I'm not hurt.'

But Timothy felt certain George was really hurt or injured in some way to cry like that, and he kept whining, and pawing at George, and trying to get on to her knee.

Julian opened the door. 'I'm going to tell Mrs Stick we want our tea,' he said, and went out. The others thought he was very brave to face Mrs Stick.

Julian went to the kitchen door and opened it. Edgar was sitting there, one side of his face scarlet, where George had slapped it. Mrs Stick was there, looking grim.

'If that girl slaps my Edgar again, I'll be after her,' she said, threateningly.

'Edgar deserved what he got,' said Julian.

'Can we have some tea, please?'

'I've a good mind to get you none,' said Mrs Stick.

Her dog started up from its corner and growled at Julian.

'That's right, Tinker! You growl at folks that slap Edgar,' said Mrs Stick.

Julian wasn't afraid of Tinker.

'If you're not going to get us any tea, I'll get it myself,' said the boy. 'Where's the bread, and where are the cakes?'

Mrs Stick stared at Julian, and the boy looked back at her steadily. He thought she was a very unpleasant woman, and he certainly wasn't going to allow her to get the better of him. He wished he could tell her to go – but he had a feeling that she wouldn't, so it would be a waste of his breath.

Mrs Stick dropped her eyes first. 'I'll get your tea,' she said, 'but if I have any nonsense from you I'll get you no other meals.'

'And if I have any nonsense from you I'll go to the police,' said Julian, unexpectedly. He hadn't meant to say that. It came out quite suddenly, but it had a surprising effect on Mrs

Stick. She looked startled and alarmed.

'Now, there's no need to be nasty,' she said in a much more polite voice. 'We've all had a bit of a shock, and we're upset, like – I'll get you your tea right now.'

Julian went out. He wondered why his sudden threat of going to the police had made Mrs Stick so much more polite. Perhaps she was afraid the police would get on to his Uncle Quentin and he'd come tearing back. Uncle Quentin wouldn't care for a hundred Mrs Sticks!

He went back to the others. 'Tea's coming,' he said. 'So cheer up, everyone!'

It wasn't a very cheerful group that sat down to the tea Mrs Stick brought in. George was now feeling ashamed of her tears. Anne was still upset. Dick tried to make a few silly jokes to cheer everyone up, but they fell so flat that he soon gave it up. Julian was grave and helpful, suddenly very grown-up.

Timothy sat close beside George, his head on her knee.

'I wish I had a dog who loved me like that,' thought Anne.

Timmy kept gazing up at George out of big,

brown, devoted eyes. He had no eyes or ears for anyone but his little mistress now she was sad.

Nobody noticed what they had for tea, but all the same it did them good, and they felt better after it. They didn't like to go out to the beach afterwards in case the phone rang, and there was news of George's mother. So they sat in the garden, keeping an ear open for the phone.

From the kitchen came a song.

*'Georgie-porgie, pudding and pie,*
*Sat herself down and had a good cry,*
*Georgie-porgie . . .'*

Julian got up. He went to the kitchen window and looked in. Edgar was there alone.

'Come out here, Edgar!' said Julian, in a grim voice. 'I'll teach you to sing another song. Come on!'

Edgar didn't stir. 'Can't I sing if I want to?' he said.

'Oh yes,' said Julian, 'but not that song. I'll teach you another. Come on out!'

'No way,' said Edgar. 'You want to fight me.'

'Yes, I do,' said Julian. 'I think a little bit of

fighting would be better for you than sitting singing nasty little songs about someone who's miserable. Are you coming out? Or shall I come in and fetch you?'

'Ma!' called Edgar, suddenly feeling panicky. 'Ma! Where are you?'

Julian suddenly reached a long arm in at the window, caught hold of Edgar's over-long nose, and pulled it so hard that Edgar yelled in pain.

'Led go! Led go! You're hurding me! Led go by dose!'

Mrs Stick came hurrying into the kitchen. She gave a scream when she saw what Julian was doing. She flew at him. Julian withdrew his arm, and stood outside the window.

'How dare you!' yelled Mrs Stick. 'First that girl slaps Edgar, and then you pull his nose! What's the matter with you all?'

'Nothing,' said Julian, pleasantly, 'but there's a lot wrong with Edgar, Mrs Stick. We feel we just *must* put it right. It should be your job, of course, but you don't seem to have done it.'

'You're downright rude,' said Mrs Stick, outraged and furious.

'Yes, I expect I am,' said Julian. 'It's just the

effect Edgar has on me. Stinker has the same effect.'

'Stinker!' cried Mrs Stick, getting angrier still. 'That's not my dog's name, and well you know it.'

'Well, it really ought to be,' said Julian, strolling off. 'Give him a bath, and maybe we'll call him Tinker instead.'

Leaving Mrs Stick muttering in fury, he went back to the others. They stared at him curiously. He somehow seemed a different Julian – a grim and determined Julian, a very grown-up Julian, a rather frightening Julian.

'I'm afraid that's done it,' said Julian, sitting down on the grass. 'I pulled Edgar's nose nearly off his fat face, and Mrs Stick saw me. I guess it's open warfare now! We won't have a very good time from now on. I doubt if we'll get any meals.'

'We'll get them ourselves then,' said George. 'I hate Mrs Stick. I wish Joanna would come back. I hate that horrible Edgar too, and that awful Stinker.'

'Look – there *is* Stinker!' suddenly said Dick, putting out his hand to catch Timothy, who had risen with a growl. But Timmy shook off his hand and leapt across the grass at once. Stinker gave a woeful howl and tried to escape. But Timothy had him by the neck and was shaking him like a rat.

Mrs Stick appeared with a stick and lashed out, not seeming to mind which dog she hit. Julian rushed for the hose again. Edgar ran indoors at once, remembering what had happened to him before.

The water gushed out, and Timothy gave a gasp and let go of the howling mongrel he held in his teeth. Stinker at once hurled himself towards Mrs Stick, and tried to hide behind her, trembling with terror.

'I'll poison that dog of yours!' said Mrs Stick, furiously, to George. 'Always setting on to mine. You look out or I'll poison him.'

She disappeared indoors, and the four children went and sat down again. George looked really worried. 'Do you suppose she really *might* try to poison Timmy?' she asked Julian, in a scared voice.

'She's a nasty bit of work,' said Julian, in a low tone. 'I think it would be just as well to keep

Timmy close by us, day and night, and only to feed him ourselves, from our own plates.'

George pulled Timothy to her, horrified at the thought that anyone might want to poison him. But Mrs Stick really was nasty – she might do anything like that, George thought. How she wished her parents were back! It was horrid to be on their own like this.

The phone rang and made everyone jump. They all leapt to their feet and Timmy growled. George flew indoors and answered the phone. She heard her father's voice, and her heart began to beat fast.

'Is that you, George?' said her father. 'Are you all right? I haven't got much time to talk.'

'Dad – what about Mum? Tell me quick – how is she?' said George.

'We won't know till the day after next,' said her father. 'I'll telephone tomorrow morning and then the next morning too. I won't come back till I know she's better.'

'Oh Dad – it's awful without you and Mum,' said poor George. 'Mrs Stick is so horrible.'

'Now, George,' said her father, rather impatiently, 'surely you children can see to yourselves and make do with Mrs Stick till I get back! Don't worry me about such things now. I've enough worry as it is.'

'When will you be back, do you think?' said George. 'Can I come and see Mum?'

'No,' said her father. 'Not for at least two weeks, they say. I'll be back as soon as I can. But I'm not going to leave your mother now. She needs me. Goodbye and be good, all of you.'

George put back the receiver. She turned to face the others.

'Won't know about Mum till the day after next,' she said. 'And we've got to put up with Mrs Stick till Dad comes back – and who knows when that will be! Isn't it awful?'

## 5 In the middle of the night

Mrs Stick was in such a bad temper that evening that there was no supper at all. Julian went to ask about some, but he found the kitchen door locked.

He went back to the others with a gloomy face, for they were all hungry.

'She's locked the door,' he said. 'She really is awful. I don't think we'll get any supper tonight.'

'We'll have to wait till she goes to bed,' said George. 'We'll go down and hunt in the larder then, and see what we can find.'

They went to bed hungry. Julian listened for Mrs Stick and Edgar to go to bed, too. When he heard them going upstairs, and was sure their doors had shut, he slipped down into the kitchen. It was dark there, and Julian was just about to put on the light when he heard the sound of someone breathing heavily. He wondered who it could be. Was it Stinker? No – it couldn't be the dog. It sounded like a human being.

Julian stood there, his hand over the light switch, puzzled and a little scared. It couldn't be a burglar, because burglars don't go to sleep in the house they have come to rob. It couldn't be Mrs Stick or Edgar. Then who was it?

He snapped on the light. The kitchen was flooded with radiance, and Julian's eyes fastened on the figure of a small man lying on the sofa. He was fast asleep, his mouth wide open.

He wasn't a very pleasant sight. He had not shaved for some days, and his cheeks and chin were bluish-black. He didn't seem to have washed for even longer than that, for his hands were black, and so were his fingernails. He had untidy hair and a nose exactly like Edgar's.

'Must be dear Edgar's father,' thought Julian to himself. 'What a sight! Well, Edgar doesn't have much of a chance with a father and mother like his.'

The man snored. Julian wondered what to do. He badly wanted to go to the larder, but on the other hand he didn't particularly want to wake up the man and have a row. He didn't see how he could turn him out – for all he knew his aunt and uncle might have agreed to Mrs Stick's husband coming there now and again, though he didn't think so.

Julian was very hungry. The thought of the good things in the larder made him snap off the light again and creep towards the larder door in the dark. He opened the door. He felt along the shelves. Good! – that felt like a pie of some sort. He lifted it up and sniffed. It smelt of meat. A meat pie – good!

He felt along the shelf again and came to a plate on which were what he thought must be jam tarts, for they were round and flat, and had something sticky in the middle. A meat pie and jam tarts ought to be all right for four hungry children!

Julian picked up the meat pie and the dish of tarts, and made his way carefully out of the larder. He pushed the door shut with his foot. Then he turned to go out of the room.

But in the dark he went the wrong way, and by bad luck walked straight into the sofa! The dish of tarts got a sudden jerk and one of them fell off. It landed on the open mouth of the sleeping man, and woke him up with a start.

'Oh no!' said Julian to himself, and began to

back away quietly, hoping that the man would turn over and go to sleep again. But the sticky jam tart sliding down his chin had startled the man, and he sat up with a jerk.

'Who's there? That you, Edgar? What are you doing down here?'

Julian said nothing but sidled towards what he hoped was the door. The man leapt up and lurched over to where he thought the light switch was. He found it and switched it on. He stared in the greatest astonishment at Julian.

'What are you doing here?' he demanded.

'Just what I was about to ask *you*,' said Julian, coolly. 'What do you think *you're* doing here, sleeping in my uncle's kitchen?'

'I've a right to be here,' said the man, in a rude voice. 'My wife's cook here, isn't she? My ship's in and I'm on leave. Your uncle arranged with my wife I could come here then, see?'

Julian had feared this might be the case. How awful to have a Mr Stick as well as a Mrs and Edgar Stick in the house! It would be completely unbearable.

'I can ask my uncle about it when he phones in the morning,' said Julian. 'Now get out of my way, please, I want to go upstairs.'

'Aha!' said Mr Stick, eyeing the meat pie and jam tarts that Julian was carrying. 'Aha! Stealing out of the larder, I see! Nice goings-on I must say.'

Julian wasn't going to argue with Mr Stick, who evidently felt that he was in charge.

'Get out of my way,' he said. 'I'll talk to you in the morning after my uncle has phoned.'

Mr Stick didn't seem as if he was going to get out of the way at all. He stood there, a nasty little man, not much taller than Julian, a sarcastic smile on his unshaven face.

Julian pursed his lips and whistled. There came a bump on the floor above. That was Timothy jumping off George's bed! Then they heard the pattering of feet down the stairs and up the kitchen passage. Timmy was coming!

He smelt Mr Stick in the doorway, put up his hackles, bared his teeth and growled. Mr Stick hastily removed himself from the doorway and then neatly banged the door in the dog's face. He grinned at Julian.

'Now what are you going to do?' he said.

'Shall I tell you?' said Julian, his temper

suddenly rising. 'I'm going to hurl this nice juicy meat pie straight into your grinning face!'

He raised his arms, and Mr Stick ducked.

'Now don't you do that,' he said. 'I'm only pulling your leg, see? Don't you waste that nice meat pie. You can go upstairs if you want to.'

He moved away to the sofa. Julian opened the door and Timothy bounded in growling. Mr Stick eyed him uncomfortably.

'Don't you let that nasty great dog come near me,' he said. 'I don't like dogs.'

'Then why don't you get rid of Stinker?' said Julian. 'Come here, Timmy! Leave him alone. He's not worth growling at.'

Julian went upstairs with Timothy close at his heels. The others crowded around him, wondering what had happened, for they had heard the voices downstairs. They laughed when Julian told them how he had nearly thrown the meat pie at Mr Stick.

'It would have served him right,' said Anne, 'though it would have been a shame, because we wouldn't have been able to eat it. Mrs Stick may be horrible, but she *can* cook. This pie is gorgeous.'

The children finished all the pie and the tarts,

too. Julian told them all about Mr Stick coming on leave from his ship.

'Three Sticks are a bit too much,' said Dick thoughtfully. 'Pity we can't get rid of them all and manage for ourselves. George, can't you persuade your dad to let us get rid of the Sticks and look after ourselves?'

'I'll try,' said George. 'You know what he's like – impossible to argue with. But I will try. Oh, I'm sleepy now. Come on, Timmy, let's get to bed! Lie on my feet. I'm hardly going to let you out of my sight now, in case those awful Sticks poison you!'

Soon the four children, now no longer hungry, were sleeping peacefully. They didn't fear the Sticks coming up to their rooms, for they knew that Timmy would wake and warn them at once. Timmy was the best guard they could have.

In the morning Mrs Stick actually produced some sort of breakfast, which surprised the children very much.

'Guess she knows your father will phone, George,' said Julian, 'and she wants to keep herself in the right. When did he say he'd call? Nine o'clock, wasn't it? Well, it's half-past eight now. Let's go for a quick run down to the beach and back.'

So off they went, the five of them, ignoring Edgar, who stood in the back garden ready to make silly faces at them. The children couldn't help thinking he must be a bit mad. He didn't act like a boy of Julian's age at all.

When they came back it was about ten minutes to nine. 'We'll sit in the sitting room till the phone rings,' said Julian. 'We don't want Mrs Stick to answer it first.'

But to their great dismay, as they reached the house, they heard Mrs Stick on the phone!

'Yes,' they heard her say, 'everything is quite all right. I can manage the children, even if they do make things a bit difficult. Yes, of course. Well it's lucky my husband is home on leave from his ship, because he can help me, like, and it makes things easier. Don't you worry about anything, and don't you bother to come back till you're ready. I'll manage everything.'

George flew into the hall like a wild thing, and snatched the phone out of Mrs Stick's hand.

'Dad! It's me, George! How's Mum? Tell me quick!'

'No worse, George,' said her father's voice. 'But we won't know anything definite till tomorrow morning. I'm glad to hear from Mrs Stick that everything is all right. I'm very upset and worried, and I'm glad to feel I can tell your mother that you're all right, and everything is going smoothly at Kirrin Cottage.'

'But it isn't,' said George, wildly. 'It isn't. It's horrible. Can't the Sticks go and let us manage things by ourselves?'

'Of course not,' said her father's voice, surprised and annoyed. 'What are you thinking of? I did hope, George, that you would be sensible and helpful. I must say . . .'

'*You* talk to him, Julian,' said George, helplessly, and thrust the phone into Julian's hand. The boy put it to his ear and spoke in his clear voice.

'Hello, this is Julian. I'm glad my aunt is no worse.'

'Well, she will be if she thinks things are going wrong at Kirrin Cottage,' said Uncle Quentin, in an exasperated voice. 'Can't you make George see reason? Can't she put up with the Sticks for a week or two? I tell you frankly, Julian, I'm not going to sack the Sticks in my absence – I want the house ready for me to bring back your aunt. If you can't put up with them, you'd better find out from your own parents if they can take you back for the rest of the holidays. But George is not to go with you. She's to stay at Kirrin Cottage. That's my last word on the subject.'

'But . . .' began Julian, wondering how he could persuade his hot-tempered uncle, 'I must tell you that . . .'

There was a click at the other end of the phone. Uncle Quentin had hung up. There was no more to be said. Julian pursed up his mouth and looked around at the others, frowning.

'He's gone!' he said. 'Cut me off just as I was trying to reason with him!'

'Serves you right!' said Mrs Stick's harsh voice from the end of the hall. 'Now you know where you stand. I'm here and I'm staying here, on your uncle's orders. And you're all going to behave yourselves, or it'll be the worse for you.'

# 6 Julian defeats the Sticks

There was a slam. The kitchen door shut, and Mrs Stick could be heard telling the news triumphantly to Edgar and Mr Stick. The children went into the sitting room, sat down and stared at one another gloomily.

'Dad's awful!' said George, furiously. 'He'll never listen to anything.'

'Well, after all, he's very upset,' said Dick, reasonably. 'It was a shame that he rang before nine, so that Mrs Stick got her say in first.'

'What did Dad say to you?' said George. 'Tell us exactly.'

'He said that if we couldn't put up with the Sticks, Anne and Dick and I were to go back to our own parents,' said Julian. 'But you were to stay here.'

George stared at Julian. 'Well,' she said at last, 'you *can't* put up with the Sticks, so you'd better all go back. I can look after myself.'

'Don't be an idiot!' said Julian, giving her arm a friendly shake. 'You know we wouldn't desert you. I can't say I look forward to the idea of being under the thumb of the Sticks for a week or two, but there are worse things than that. We'll "stick" it together.'

But his feeble joke didn't raise a smile, even from Anne. The idea of being under the Sticks' three thumbs was very unpleasant. Timothy put his head on George's knee. She patted him and looked around.

'You go back home,' she said to the others. 'I've got a plan of my own, and you're not in it. I've got Timmy, and he'll look after me. Phone your parents and go home tomorrow.'

George stared around defiantly. Her head was up, and there was no doubt but that she had made a plan of some sort.

Julian felt uneasy.

'Don't be silly,' he said. 'I tell you we're all together in this. If you've got a plan, we'll come into it. But we're staying here with you, whatever happens.'

'Stay if you like,' said George, 'but my plan goes on, and you'll find you'll have to go home in the end. Come on, Timothy! Let's go to Jim and see if my boat is ready.'

'We'll go with you,' said Dick. He was sorry for George. He could see behind her attitude, and he knew she was very unhappy, worried about her mother, angry with her father, and upset because she felt the others were staying on because of her, when they could go back home and have a lovely time.

It wasn't a happy day. George was very prickly, and kept on insisting that the others should go back home and leave her. She got quite angry when they were just as insistent that they wouldn't.

'You're spoiling my plan,' she said at last. 'You *should* go back, you really should. I tell you, you're spoiling my plan completely.'

'Well, what *is* your plan?' said Julian impatiently. 'I can't help feeling you're just *pretending* you've got a plan, so that we'll go.'

'I'm *not* pretending,' said George, losing her temper. 'Do I ever pretend? You know I don't! If I say I've got a plan, I *have* got a plan. But I'm not giving it away, so it's no good asking me. It's my own secret, private plan.'

'I do think you could tell us,' said Dick, quite hurt. 'After all, we're your best friends, aren't we? And we're going to stick by you, plan or no plan – yes, even if we spoil your plan, as you say, we'll still stay here with you.'

'I won't *let* you spoil my plan,' said George, her eyes flashing. 'You're mean. You're against me, just like the Sticks are.'

'Oh, George, don't,' said Anne, almost in tears. 'Don't let's argue. It's bad enough dealing with those awful Sticks, without *us* arguing too.'

George's temper died down as quickly as it had risen. She looked ashamed.

'Sorry!' she said. 'I'm an idiot. I won't argue. But I do mean what I say. I'll go on with my plan, and I won't tell you what it is, because if I do, it will spoil the holidays for you. Please believe me.'

'Let's take our dinner out with us again,' said Julian, getting up. 'We'll all feel better away from this house today. I'll go and tackle the old Stick.'

'Isn't he brave!' said Anne, who would rather have died than go and face Mrs Stick at that moment.

Mrs Stick proved very difficult. She felt rather victorious at the time, and was also very annoyed to find that her beautiful meat pie and jam tarts had disappeared. Mr Stick was in the middle of telling her where they had gone when Julian appeared.

'How you can expect sandwiches for a picnic when you've stolen my meat pie and jam tarts, I *don't* know!' she began, indignantly. 'You can have dry bread and jam for your picnic, and that's all. And what's more, I wouldn't give you that either except that I'm glad to be rid of you.'

'Good riddance to bad rubbish,' murmured Edgar to himself. He was lying sprawled on the sofa, reading some kind of highly coloured comic.

'If you've anything to say to me, Edgar, come outside and say it,' said Julian, dangerously.

'You leave Edgar alone,' said Mrs Stick, at once.

'There's nothing I'd like better,' said Julian, scornfully. 'Who wants to be with him? Cowardly little spotty-face!'

'Now, now, look 'ere!' began Mr Stick, from his corner.

'I don't want to look at you,' said Julian at once.

'Now, look *'ere*,' said Mr Stick, angrily, standing up.

'I've told you I don't want to,' said Julian. 'You're not a pleasant sight.'

'*Cheek*!' said Mrs Stick, rapidly losing her temper.

'No, not cheek – just the plain truth,' said Julian, airily. Mrs Stick glared at him. Julian defeated her. He had such a quick tongue, and he said everything so politely. The ruder his words were, the more politely he spoke. Mrs Stick didn't understand people like Julian. She felt that they were too clever for her. She disliked the boy, and banged a saucepan noisily down on the sink.

Stinker jumped up and growled at the sudden noise.

'Hello, Stinker!' said Julian. 'Had a bath yet? No! – as smelly as ever, aren't you?'

'You know that dog's name isn't Stinker,' said Mrs Stick, angrily. 'You get out of my kitchen.'

'Right!' said Julian. 'Pleased to go. Don't bother about the dry bread and jam. I'll manage something a bit better than that.'

He went out, whistling. Stinker growled, and Edgar repeated loudly what he had said before: 'Good riddance to bad rubbish!'

'What did you say?' said Julian, suddenly poking his head in at the kitchen door again. But Edgar didn't dare to repeat it, so off went Julian again, whistling cheerfully, but not feeling nearly as cheerful as his whistle. He was worried. After all, if Mrs Stick was going to make meals as difficult as this, life wasn't going to be very pleasant at Kirrin Cottage.

'Anyone fancy dry bread and jam for lunch?' inquired Julian, when he returned to the others. 'No? I thought not, so I turned down Mrs Stick's kind offer. I vote we go and buy something decent. That shop in the village has good sausage rolls.'

George had been very silent all morning. She was worrying about her mother, the others knew. She was probably thinking about her plan too, they thought, and wondered what it could be.

'Shall we go over to Kirrin Island today?' asked Julian, thinking that it would take George's mind off her worries if they went to her beloved island.

George shook her head.

'No,' she said. 'I don't feel like it. The boat's all ready, I know – but I just don't feel like it. Till I know Mum is going to get better, I don't want to be out of reach of the house. If Dad called, the Sticks could always send Edgar to look for me – and if I was on the island, he couldn't find me.'

The children messed about that day, doing nothing at all. They went back to tea, and Mrs Stick provided them with bread and butter and jam, but no cake. The milk was sour, so everyone had to have tea without milk, which they all disliked.

As they ate their tea, the children heard Edgar outside the window. He held a tin bowl in his hand, and put it down on the grass outside.

'Your dog's dinner,' he yelled.

'He looks like a dog's dinner himself,' said Dick, in disgust.

That made everyone laugh. 'Edgar, the Dog's Dinner!' said Anne. 'Any biscuits in that tin on the sideboard, do you think, George?'

George got up to see. Timothy slipped out and went to the dish put down for him. He sniffed at it. George, coming back from the sideboard, looked out of the window as she passed and saw him. At once the thought of poison came back to her mind and she yelled to Timothy, making the others jump out of their skins.

'Tim! Tim! Don't touch it!'

Timothy wagged his tail as if to say he didn't mean to touch it, anyway. George rushed out and picked up the bowl of raw meat. She sniffed at it.

'You haven't touched it, have you, Timothy?' she said, anxiously.

Dick leaned out of the window.

'No, he didn't eat any. I watched him. He sniffed it, but he wouldn't touch it. I bet it's been dosed with rat poison or something.'

George was very white. 'Oh Timmy!' she said. 'You're such a sensible dog. You wouldn't touch poisoned stuff, would you?'

'Woof!' said Timmy, decidedly. Stinker heard the bark and put his nose out of the kitchen door.

George called to him in a loud voice:

'Stinker, Stinker, come here! Timmy doesn't want his dinner. You can have it. Come along, Stinker, here it is!'

Edgar came rushing out behind Stinker. 'Don't you give that to him,' he said.

'Why not?' asked George. 'Go on, Edgar – tell me why not.'

'He doesn't eat raw meat,' said Edgar, after a

pause. 'He only eats dog biscuits.'

'That's a lie!' said George, flaring up. 'I saw him eating meat yesterday. Here, Stinker – you come and eat this.'

Edgar snatched the bowl from George, almost snarling at her, and ran indoors at top speed. George was about to go after him, but Julian, who had jumped out of the window when Edgar came up, stopped her.

'No point!' he said. 'You won't get anything out of him. The meat's probably in the bin by now. From now on, we feed Timothy ourselves with meat bought from the butcher with our own money. Don't be afraid that he'll eat poisoned stuff. He's too wise a dog for that.'

'He might, if he was really, really hungry, Julian,' said George, looking a bit green. She felt sick inside. 'I wasn't going to let Stinker eat that poisoned stuff, of course, but I guessed that if it *was* poisoned, one of the Sticks would come rushing out and stop Stinker eating it. And Edgar did. So it proves it was poisoned, doesn't it?'

'I think it probably does,' said Julian. 'But don't worry, George. Timmy won't be poisoned.'

'But he might, he might,' said George, putting

her hand on the big dog's head. 'I can't bear the thought of it, Julian. I really can't.'

'Don't think about it then,' said Julian, taking her indoors again. 'Here, have a biscuit!'

'You don't think the Sticks would poison *us*, do you?' said Anne, looking suddenly scared and gazing at her biscuit as if it might bite her.

'No, idiot. They only want to get Timmy out of the way because he guards us so well,' said Julian. 'Don't look so scared. All this will settle down in a day or two, and we'll have a good time after all. You'll see!'

But Julian only said this to comfort his little sister. Secretly he was very worried. He wished he could take Anne, Dick and George back to his own home. But he knew George wouldn't come. And how could they leave her to the Sticks? It was impossible. Friends had to stick together, and somehow they had to cope until Aunt Fanny and Uncle Quentin came back.

## 7 *Better news*

'Do you think we'd better slip down after the Sticks have gone to bed and get some food out of the larder again?' said Dick, when no supper appeared that evening.

Julian didn't fancy sneaking down and confronting Mr Stick again. Not that he was afraid of him, but the whole thing was so unpleasant. This was their house, the food was theirs – so why should they have to beg for it, or take it on the sly? It was ridiculous.

'Come here, Timothy!' said Julian. The dog left George's side and went to Julian, looking up at the boy enquiringly. 'You're going to come with me and persuade dear kind Mrs Stick to give us the best things out of the larder!' said Julian, with a grin.

The others laughed, cheering up at once.

'Good idea!' said Dick. 'Can we all come and see the fun?'

'Better not,' said Julian. 'I can manage fine by myself.'

He went down the passage to the kitchen. The radio was on inside, so no one in the kitchen heard Julian till he was actually standing inside the room. Then Edgar looked up and saw Timothy as well as Julian.

Edgar was scared of the big dog, who was now growling fiercely. He went behind the kitchen sofa and stayed there, eyeing Timmy fearfully.

'What do you want?' said Mrs Stick, turning off the radio.

'Supper,' said Julian, pleasantly. 'Supper! The best things out of the larder – bought with my uncle's money, cooked on my aunt's stove with gas she pays for – yes, supper! Open the larder door and let's see what there is in there.'

'Well, of all the nerve!' began Mr Stick, in amazement.

'You can have a loaf of bread and some cheese,' said Mrs Stick, 'and that's my last word.'

'Well, it isn't my last word,' said Julian, and he went to the larder door. 'Timmy, keep to heel! Growl all you like, but don't bite anybody – yet!'

Timmy's growls were really frightening. Even Mr Stick put himself at the other end of the room. As for Stinker, he was nowhere to be seen. He had backed away at the very first growl, and was now shivering in the corner.

Mrs Stick's mouth went into a hard straight line. 'You take the bread and cheese and clear out,' she said.

Julian opened the larder door, whistling softly, which annoyed Mrs Stick more than anything else.

'Excellent!' said Julian, admiringly. 'You certainly know how to stock a larder, Mrs Stick. A roast chicken! I thought I smelt one cooking. I suppose Mr Stick killed one of our chickens today. I thought I heard a lot of squawking. And what enormous tomatoes! Best to be got from the village, I expect. Oh, Mrs Stick – what a delicious-looking treacle tart! I must say, you're a very good cook.'

Julian picked up the chicken and the dish of tomatoes, and then balanced the plate with the treacle tart on the top.

Mrs Stick yelled at him.

'You leave those things alone! That's our

supper! You leave them there.'

'You've made a little mistake,' said Julian, politely. 'It's *our* supper! We've had very little to eat today, and we could do with a good supper. Thanks very much!'

'Now look 'ere!' began Mr Stick, angrily, furious at seeing his lovely supper walking away.

'Surely you don't want me to look at you *again*?' said Julian, in a tone of amazement. 'What for? Have you shaved yet – or washed? I'm afraid not. So, if you don't mind I think I'd rather *not* look at you.'

Mr Stick was speechless. He wasn't quick with his tongue, and a boy like Julian took his breath away, and left him with nothing to say except his favourite 'Now, look 'ere!'

'Put those things down,' said Mrs Stick sharply. 'What do you think we're going to have for *our* supper if you walk off with them? You tell me that!'

'Easy!' said Julian. 'Let me offer you our supper – bread and cheese, Mrs Stick, bread and cheese!'

Mrs Stick made an angry noise, and started to go after Julian with her hand raised. But Timothy immediately leapt at her, and his teeth snapped together with a loud click.

'Oh!' howled Mrs Stick. 'That dog of yours nearly took my hand off! I'll do for him one day, you see if I don't.'

'You had a good try today, didn't you?' said Julian, in a quiet voice, fixing his eyes straight on the woman's face. 'That's a matter for the police, isn't it? Be careful, Mrs Stick. I've a good mind to go to the police tomorrow.'

Just as before, the mention of the police seemed to frighten Mrs Stick. She cast a look at her husband and took a step backwards. Julian wondered if the man had done something wrong and was hiding from the police. He never seemed to put a foot outside.

The boy went up the passage triumphantly. Timmy followed at his heels, disappointed that he hadn't been able to get a nibble at Stinker. Julian marched into the sitting room, and set the dishes carefully down on the table.

'Look what *I've* got!' he said. 'The Sticks' own supper!'

He told the others what had happened, and they laughed loudly.

'How do you think of all those things to say?' said Anne, admiringly. 'I'm not surprised you make them so angry, Ju. It's a good thing we've got Timmy to back us up.'

'Yes, I wouldn't feel nearly so brave without Timmy,' said Julian.

It was a very good supper. There were knives and forks in the sideboard, and the children made do with fruit plates from the sideboard too, rather than go and get plates from the kitchen. There was bread left over from their tea, so they were able to make a very good meal. They enjoyed it thoroughly.

'Sorry we can't give you the chicken bones, Tim,' said George, 'but they might splinter inside you and hurt you. You can have all the scraps. Don't leave any for Stinker!'

Timmy didn't. With two or three great gulps he cleared his plate, and then sat waiting for any scraps of treacle tart that might descend his way.

The children felt happy after such a good meal. They had completely eaten the chicken. Nothing was left except a pile of bones. They had eaten all the tomatoes too, finished the bread, and enjoyed every scrap of the treacle tart.

It was late. Anne yawned, and then George yawned too.

'Let's go to bed,' she said. 'I don't feel like having a game of cards or anything.'

So they went to bed, and as usual Timothy lay heavily on George's feet. He lay there awake for some time, his ears cocked to hear noises from below. He heard the Sticks go up to bed. He heard doors closing. He heard a whine from Stinker. Then all was silence. Timmy dropped his head on to his paws and slept – but he kept one ear cocked for danger. Timothy didn't trust the Sticks any more than the children did!

The children awoke very early in the morning. Julian awoke first. It was a beautiful day. Julian went to the window and looked out. The sky was a very pale blue, and rosy-pink clouds floated above. The sea was a clear blue too, smooth and calm. Julian remembered what Anne often said – that the world in the early morning always looked as if it had just been washed – so clean and new and fresh!

The children all had a swim before breakfast, and this time they were back at half-past eight, afraid that George's father might phone early again. Julian saw Mrs Stick on the stairs and called to her.

'Has my uncle phoned yet?'

'No,' said the woman, in a surly tone. She had been hoping that the phone would ring while the children were out, then, as she had done the day before, she could answer it, and get a few words in first.

'We'll have breakfast now, please,' said Julian. 'A *good* breakfast, Mrs Stick. My uncle *might* ask us what we'd had for breakfast, mightn't he? You never know.'

Mrs Stick evidently thought that Julian might tell his uncle if she gave them only bread and butter for breakfast, so very soon the children smelt a delicious smell of bacon frying. Mrs Stick brought in a dish of it garnished with tomatoes. She banged it down on the table with the plates. Edgar arrived with a pot of tea and a tray of cups and saucers.

'Ah, here's Edgar!' said Julian, in a tone of friendly surprise. 'Dear old spotty-face!'

'Garn!' said Edgar, and banged down the teapot. Timmy growled, and Edgar fled for his life.

George didn't want any breakfast. Julian put

hers back in the warm dish and put a plate over it. He knew that she was waiting for news. If only the phone would ring – then she would know if her mother was really better or not.

It did ring as they were halfway through the meal. George was there before the end of the first ring.

'Dad! Yes, it's George. How's Mum?'

There was a pause as George listened. All the children stopped eating and listened in silence, waiting for George to speak. They would know by her next words if the news was good or not.

'Oh – oh, I'm so glad!' they heard George say. 'Did she have the operation yesterday? Oh, you never told me! But it's all right now, is it? Poor Mum! Give her my love. I really want to see her. Oh Dad, can't I come?'

Evidently the answer was no. George listened for a while then spoke a few more words and said goodbye.

She ran into the sitting room.

'You heard, didn't you?' she said, joyfully. 'Mum's better. She'll get well now, and she'll be back home soon – in about ten days. Dad won't come back till he brings her home. It's good news about Mum – but I'm afraid we can't get rid of the Sticks.'

## 8 George's plan

Mrs Stick had overheard the conversation on the telephone – at least, she had heard George's side of it. She knew that George's mother was better and that her father would not return till her mother could be brought home. That would be in about ten days! The Sticks could have a good time till then, no doubt about that!

George suddenly found that her appetite had come back. She ate her bacon hungrily, and scraped the dish around with a piece of bread. She had three cups of tea, and then sat back contentedly.

'I feel better,' she said. Anne slipped her hand in hers. She was very glad that her aunt was going to be all right. If it wasn't for the horrible Sticks they could have a lovely time. Then George said something that made Julian cross.

'Well, now that I know Mum is going to be better, I can stand up to the Sticks all right by myself with Timmy. So I want you three to go

back home and finish the holidays without me.
I'll be all right.'

'Shut up, George,' said Julian. 'We've argued
this all out before. I've made up my mind – and
I don't change it, any more than *you* do, when
I've made it up.'

'I told you I'd got a plan,' said George, 'and
you don't come into it, I'm afraid. You'll have to
go back home whether you want to or not.'

'Don't be so mysterious, George!' said Julian,
impatiently. 'What is this plan? You'd better tell
us, even if we're not in it. Can't you trust us?'

'Yes, of course. But you might try to stop me,'
said George, looking sulky.

'Then you'd definitely better tell us,' said Julian
feeling worried.

George could be so reckless once she got ideas
into her head. She might do anything!

But George wouldn't say another word. Julian
gave up at last, but secretly made up his mind not
to let George out of his sight that day. If she was
going to carry out some crazy plan, then she
would have to do it under his eye!

But George didn't seem to be carrying out any
plan. She swam again with the others, went out

for a walk with them, and went for a row on the sea. She didn't want to go to Kirrin Island, so the others didn't press her, thinking that she didn't want to be out of sight of the beach in case Edgar came with a message from her father.

It was quite a happy day. The children bought sausage rolls again, and fruit, and picnicked on the beach. Timmy had a large and juicy bone from the butcher's.

'I've got a bit of shopping to do,' said George, about tea-time. 'Go and see if Mrs Stick is getting some tea for us, and I'll fly down to the shops and get what I want.'

Julian pricked up his ears at once. Was George sending them off so that she could be alone to carry out this mysterious plan of hers?

'I'll come with you,' said Julian, getting up. 'Dick can tackle Mrs Stick for once, and take Timmy with him.'

'No, you go,' said George. 'I won't be long.'

But Julian was determined not to go. In the end they all went with George, as Dick didn't want to face Mrs Stick without Julian or George.

George went into the little general shop and got a new battery for her torch. She bought two boxes of matches and a bottle of methylated spirit.

'What do you want that for?' said Anne in surprise.

'Oh, it might come in useful,' said George, and said no more.

They all went back to Kirrin Cottage. Tea was actually on the table! True, it wasn't a wonderful tea, being merely bread and jam and a pot of hot tea – still it was there, and was edible.

It rained that evening. The children sat around the table and played cards. They all felt happier now that they had had good news of George's mother. In the middle of the game Julian got up and rang the bell. The others stared at him in surprise.

'What are you ringing the bell for?' asked George, her eyes wide with astonishment.

'To tell Mrs Stick to bring some supper,' said Julian, with a grin. But no one answered the bell. So Julian rang again and then again.

The kitchen door opened at last and Mrs Stick came up the passage, evidently in a bad temper. She came into the sitting room.

'You stop ringing that bell!' she said, angrily.

'I'm not answering any bells rung by you.'

'I rang it to tell you that we wanted some supper,' said Julian. 'And to say that if you would rather I came and got it myself from the larder – with Timmy – as I did last night, that's fine. But if not, you can bring a decent supper to us yourself.'

'If you come stealing things out of my larder again, I'll – I'll . . .' began Mrs Stick.

'You'll call in the police!' Julian finished for her. 'Do. That would suit us. I can just imagine our local policeman taking down all the details in his notebook. I could give him quite a few.'

Mrs Stick muttered something rude under her breath, glared at Julian as if she could kill him, and went off down the passage again. By the sound of the clattering and crashing of crockery in the kitchen it was plain that Mrs Stick was getting some sort of supper for them, and Julian grinned to himself as he dealt out the cards.

Supper wasn't as good as the night before, but it wasn't bad. It was a little cold ham, cheese and the remains of a milk pudding. There was also a plate of cooked meat for Timmy.

George looked at it sharply. 'Take that away,'

she said. 'I bet you've poisoned it again. Take it away!'

'No, leave it here,' said Julian. 'I'll take it down to the chemist tomorrow and get him to test it. If it's poisoned, the chemist might have a lot of interesting things to tell us.'

Mrs Stick took the meat away without a word.

'Horrible woman!' said George, pulling Timothy close to her. 'I hate her! I feel so afraid for Timmy.'

Somehow that spoilt the evening. As it grew dark the children became sleepy.

'It's ten o'clock,' said Julian. 'Bedtime! Anne ought to have gone long ago. She isn't old enough to stay up as late as this.'

'*Hey*!' said Anne, indignantly. 'I'm nearly as old as George, aren't I? I can't help being younger, can I?'

'All right, all right!' said Julian, laughing. 'I won't make you go off to bed by yourself, don't worry. We all stay together in this house while the Sticks are about. Come on! Let's all go to bed now.'

They were all tired. They had swum, walked and rowed that day. Julian tried to keep awake a little while, but he too fell asleep very quickly.

He awoke with a jump, thinking that he had heard a noise. But everything was quiet. What could the noise have been? Was it one of the Sticks creeping about? No – it couldn't be that, or Tim would have barked the house down. Then what was it? *Something* must have woken him.

'I wonder if it's George carrying out that plan of hers!' thought Julian, suddenly. He sat up. He felt about for his dressing gown and put it on. Without waking Dick he crept to the girls' room, and switched on his torch to see that they were all right.

Anne was in her bed, sleeping peacefully. But George's bed was empty. George's clothes were gone!

'Oh no!' said Julian, under his breath. 'Where has she gone? I bet she's run away to find where her mother is!'

His torch picked out a white envelope pinned to George's pillow. He stepped softly over to it.

It had his name printed on it in bold letters. 'Julian.' Julian ripped it open and read it.

'Dear Julian,' said the note,

'Don't be angry with me, please. I daren't stay in Kirrin Cottage any longer in case the Sticks somehow poison Timmy. You know that would break my heart. So I've gone to live by myself on our island till Mum and Dad come back. Please leave a note for Dad and tell him to ask Jim to sail near Kirrin Island with his little red flag flying from the mast as soon as they're back. Then I'll come home. You and Dick and Anne should go home now I've gone. It'd be silly to stay at Kirrin Cottage with the Sticks now I'm not there.

Love from

GEORGE.'

Julian read the note through. 'Well, why didn't I guess that was her plan!' he said to himself. 'That's why we didn't come into it! She meant to go off by herself with Timmy. I can't let her do that. She can't live all by herself on Kirrin Island for so long. She might fall ill. She might slip on a rock and hurt herself, and no one would ever know!'

The boy was really worried about his determined cousin. He wondered what to do. That noise he heard must have been made by George, so she couldn't have much of a head start. If he ran down to the beach, George might still be there, and he could stop her.

So, in his dressing gown, he ran down the front path, out of the gate, and took the road to the beach. The rain had stopped, and the stars were out. But it wasn't a light night.

'How can George expect to get through those rocks in the dark?' he thought. 'She's mad! She'll hit her boat on a rock, and sink.'

He raced on in the darkness, talking aloud to himself. 'No wonder she wanted a new battery for her torch, and matches – and I suppose the methylated spirit was for her little cooking stove! Why couldn't she tell us? It would have been fun to go with her.'

He came to the beach. He saw the light of a torch where George kept her boat. He ran to it, his feet sinking in the soft wet sand.

'George! Idiot! You can't go off like this all alone, in the middle of the night!' called Julian.

George was pushing her boat out into the water.

She jumped when she heard Julian's voice.

'You can't stop me!' she said.

But Julian caught hold of the boat, as he waded up to his waist in the water. 'George, listen to me! You can't go like this. You'll hit a rock. Come back!'

'No,' said George, getting cross. 'You can go back home, Julian. I'll be all right. Let go of my boat!'

'George, why didn't you tell me your plan?' said Julian, almost swept off his feet by a wave. 'These waves are really big! I'll have to get into the boat.'

He climbed in. He couldn't see George, but he felt certain that she was glaring at him. Timmy licked his wet legs.

'You're spoiling everything,' said George, with a break in her voice that meant she was upset.

'I'm not, silly!' said Julian, in a gentle voice. 'Listen! – you come back to Kirrin Cottage with me now, George, and I promise you something. Tomorrow we'll *all* go to the island with you. The whole lot of us. Why shouldn't we? Your mother said we could spend a week there, anyway, didn't she? We'll be out of the reach of those horrible Sticks. We'll have a brilliant time. So will you come back now, George, and let us go together tomorrow?'

# 9 *An exciting night*

There was a silence, except for the waves splashing around the boat. Then George's voice came out of the darkness, lifted joyfully.

'Oh Julian – do you mean it? Will you really come with me? I was afraid I'd get into trouble for doing this, because Dad said I had to stay at Kirrin Cottage till he came back – and you know how he hates disobedience. But I knew if I stayed there, you would too – and I didn't want you to be miserable with those horrid Sticks – so I thought I'd come away. I didn't think you'd come too, because of getting into trouble! I never even thought of asking you.'

'You're very stupid sometimes, aren't you, George?' said Julian. 'As if we'd care about getting into trouble, so long as we were all together! Of course we'll come with you – and I'll take all the responsibility for this escape, and tell your father it's my fault.'

'Oh no you won't,' said George, quickly. 'I'll say it was my idea. If I do wrong, I'm not afraid to own up to it. You know that.'

'Well, we won't argue that now,' said Julian. 'We'll have at least a week or ten days on Kirrin Island to do all the arguing we want to. The thing is – let's get back now, wake up the others for a bit, and have a nice quiet talk about this plan of yours. I think it's a very, very good idea!'

George was overjoyed. 'I feel as if I could hug you, Julian,' she said. 'Where are the oars? Oh, here they are! The boat's floated quite a long way out.'

She rowed strongly back to the shore. Julian jumped out and pulled the boat up the beach, with George's help. He shone his torch into the boat.

'You've got a good stash of things here,' he said. 'Bread and ham and butter and stuff. How did you manage to get them without Mr Stick seeing you tonight? I suppose you slipped down and got them out of the larder?'

'Yes, I did,' said George. 'But there was no one in the kitchen tonight. Perhaps Mr Stick has gone to sleep upstairs. Or maybe he has gone back to his ship. Anyway, there was no one there when I crept down, not even Stinker.'

'We'd better leave them here,' said Julian. 'Stuff them into that locker and shut the lid. No one will guess there's anything there. We'll have to bring down a lot more stuff if we're all going to live on the island. This is going to be fun!'

They made their way back to the house, feeling very excited. Julian's wet dressing gown flapped around his legs, and he pulled it up high to be out of the way. Timothy gambolled around, not seeming at all surprised at the night's events.

When they got back to the house they woke the other two, who listened in astonishment to what had happened that night. Anne was so excited to think that they were all going to live on the island that she raised her voice in joy.

'That's the loveliest thing that could happen! I think . . .'

'Shut up!' said three furious voices in loud whispers. 'You'll wake the Sticks!'

'Sorry!' whispered Anne. 'But it's so exciting!'

They began to discuss the plans.

'If we go for a week or ten days, we must take plenty of supplies,' said Julian. 'The thing is – can we find enough food for that long? Even if we entirely empty the larder I doubt it'd be enough for a week or so. We're all such hungry people.'

'Julian,' said George, suddenly remembering something, '*I* know what we'll do! Mum has a store cupboard in her room. She keeps dozens and dozens of tins of food there, in case we ever get snowed in during winter, and can't go to the village. That's happened once or twice. And I know where Mum keeps the key! Can't we open the cupboard and get out some tins?'

'Of course!' said Julian, delighted. 'I know Aunt Fanny wouldn't mind. And anyway, we can make a list of what we take and replace them for her, if she does mind. It will be my birthday soon, and I'm sure to get money then.'

'Where's the key?' whispered Dick.

'Let's go into Mum's room, and I'll show you where she keeps it,' said George. 'I just hope she hasn't taken it with her.'

But George's mother had felt far too ill when she left home to think of cupboard keys. George fumbled at the back of a drawer in the dressing table and brought out two or three keys tied together with thin string. She fitted first one and then another into a cupboard in the wall. The second one opened the door.

Julian shone his torch into the cupboard. It was filled with tins of food of all kinds, neatly arranged on the shelves.

'Perfect!' said Dick, his eyes gleaming. 'Soup – tins of meat – tins of fruit – tinned milk – sardines – tinned butter – biscuits – tinned vegetables! There's everything we want here!'

'Yes,' said Julian, pleased. 'It's great. We'll take all we can carry. Is there a bag or two anywhere about, George, do you know?'

Soon the tins were quietly packed into two bags. The cupboard door was shut and locked again. The children crept to their own rooms once more.

'Well, that's the biggest problem solved – food,' said Julian. 'We'll raid the larder too, and take what bread there is – and cake. What about water, George? Is there any on the island?'

'Well, I suppose there's some in that old well,' said George, thinking, 'but as there's no bucket or anything, we can't get any. I was taking a big container of fresh water with me – but we'd better fill two or three more now you're all coming! I know where there are some, quite clean and new.'

So they filled some containers with fresh water, and put them with the bags, ready to take to the boat. It was so exciting doing all these things in the middle of the night! Anne could hardly keep her voice down to a whisper, and it was a wonder that Timothy didn't bark, for he sensed the excitement of the others.

There was a tin of cakes in the larder, freshly made, so those were added to the heap that was forming in the front garden. There was a large joint of meat too, and George wrapped it in a cloth and put that with the heap, telling Timmy in a fierce voice that if he so much as sniffed at it she would leave him behind!

'I've got my little stove for boiling water on, or heating up anything,' whispered George. 'It's in the boat. That's what I bought the methylated spirits for, of course. You didn't guess, did you? And the matches for lighting it. What about candles? We can't use our torches all the time, the batteries would soon run out.'

They found a packet of candles in the kitchen cupboard, a kettle, a saucepan, some old knives and forks and spoons, and several other things they thought they might want. They also came across some small bottles of ginger beer, evidently stored for their own use by the Sticks.

'All bought with my mum's money!' said George. 'Well, we'll take the ginger beer too. It'll be nice to drink it on a hot day.'

'Where are we going to sleep at night?' said Julian. 'In that ruined part of the old castle, where there's just one room with a roof left, and walls?'

'That's where I planned to sleep,' said George. 'I was going to make a bed out of some of the heather that grows on the island, covered by a rug or two, which I've got down in the boat.'

'We'll take all the rugs we can find,' said Julian. 'And some cushions for pillows. Isn't this fun? I don't know when I've felt so excited. I feel like a prisoner escaping to freedom! Won't the Sticks be amazed when they find us gone!'

'Yes – we'll have to decide what to say to them,' said George, looking serious. 'We don't want them sending people after us to the island, making us come back. I don't think they should know we've gone there.'

'We'll discuss that later,' said Dick. 'The thing is to get everything to the boat while it's dark. It'll soon be dawn.'

'How are we going to get all this down to George's boat?' said Anne, looking at the enormous pile of goods by the light of her torch. 'We'll never be able to carry them all!'

It certainly was a huge pile. Julian had an idea, as usual.

'Are there any wheelbarrows in the shed?' he asked George. 'If we could pile the things into a couple of wheelbarrows, we could easily take everything in one journey. We could wheel them along on the sandy side of the road so that we don't make any noise.'

'Oh, good idea!' said George. 'I wish I'd thought of that before. I had to make about five journeys to and from the boat when I took my own things. There are two wheelbarrows in the shed. We'll get them. One has a squeaky wheel, but let's hope no one hears it.'

Stinker heard the squeak, as he lay in a corner of Mrs Stick's room. He pricked up his ears and growled softly. He didn't dare to bark, for he was afraid of bringing Timothy up. Mrs Stick didn't hear the growl. She slept soundly, not even stirring. She had no idea what was going on downstairs.

The things were all stowed into the boat. The children didn't like leaving them there unguarded. In the end they decided to leave Dick there, sleeping on the rugs. They stood thinking for a moment before they went back without Dick.

'I hope we've remembered everything,' said George, wrinkling up her forehead. 'Oh – I know! We haven't remembered a tin opener – or a bottle opener to take off the tops of the ginger-beer bottles.'

'We'll put those in our pockets when we get back to the house and find them,' said Julian. 'I remember seeing some in the sideboard drawer. Bye, Dick. We'll be down very early to row off. We must get some bread at the baker's as soon as he opens, because we've got hardly any, and we'll see if we can pick up a very large bone at the butcher's for Timmy. George has got a bag of biscuits in the boat for him too.'

The three of them set off back to the house with Timmy, leaving Dick curled up comfortably on the rugs. He soon fell asleep again, his face upturned to the stars that would soon fade from the sky.

The others talked about what to tell the Sticks. 'I think we shouldn't tell them anything,' said Julian, at last. 'I don't particularly want to tell them deliberate lies, and I'm certainly not going to tell them the truth. I know what we'll do – there's a train that leaves the station about eight o'clock, which would be the one we'd catch if we were going home. We'll find a timetable, leave it open on the dining-room table, as if we'd been looking up a train, and then we'll all set off across the moor at the back of the house, as if we were going to the station.'

'Oh yes – then the Sticks will think we've run away, and gone to catch the train back home,' said Anne. 'They will never guess we've gone to the island.'

'That's a good idea,' said George, pleased. 'But how will we know when Dad and Mum get back?'

'Is there anyone you could leave a message with – somebody you could really trust?' asked Julian.

George thought hard. 'There's Alf the fisherman's son,' she said at last. 'He used to look after Tim for me when I wasn't allowed to have him in the house. I know he wouldn't give us away.'

'We'll call on Alf before we go then,' said Julian. 'Now, let's look for that timetable and lay it open on the table at the right place.'

They hunted for the timetable, found the right page, and underlined the train they hoped that the Sticks would think they were catching. They found the tin and bottle openers and put them into their pockets. Julian found two or three more boxes of matches too. He thought two would not last long enough.

By this time dawn had come and the house was being flooded with early sunshine. 'I wonder if the bakery is open,' said Julian. 'We might as well go and see. It's about six o'clock.'

They went to the bakery. It wasn't open, but the new loaves had already been made. The baker was outside, sunning himself. He had baked his bread at night, ready to sell it new-made in the morning. He grinned at the children.

'Up early today,' he said. 'What, you want some of my loaves – how many? Six! Good heavens, whatever for?'

'To eat,' said George, grinning.

Julian paid for six enormous loaves, and they went to the butcher's. His shop wasn't open either, but the butcher was sweeping the path outside.

'Could we buy a very big bone for Timmy, please?' asked George.

She got an enormous one, and Timmy looked at it longingly. Such a bone would last him for days, he knew!

'Now,' said Julian, as they set off to the boat, 'we'll pack these things into the boat, then go back to the house, and make a noise so that the Sticks know we're there. Then we'll set off across the moors, and hope the Sticks will think we're making for the train.'

They woke Dick, who was still sleeping peacefully in the boat, and packed in the bread and bone.

'Take the boat into the next cove,' said George. 'Can you do that? We'll be hidden from anyone on the beach then. The fishermen are all out in their boats, fishing. We won't be seen, if we set off in about an hour's time. We'll be back by then.'

They went back to the house and made a noise as if they were just getting up. George whistled to

Timmy, and Julian sang at the top of his voice. Then, with a great banging of doors, they set out down the path and cut across the moors, in full sight of the kitchen window.

'Hope the Sticks won't notice Dick isn't with us,' said Julian, seeing Edgar staring out of the window. 'I expect they'll think he's gone ahead.'

They kept to the path until they came to a dip, where they were hidden from any watcher at Kirrin Cottage. Then they took another path that led them, unseen, to the cove where Dick had taken the boat. He was there, waiting anxiously for them.

'Here we are!' yelled Julian, in excitement. 'The adventure is about to begin.'

## 10  Kirrin Island once more!

They all clambered into the boat. Timothy leapt in lightly and ran to the prow, where he always stood. His tongue hung out in excitement. He knew quite well that something was up – and he was in it! No wonder he panted and wagged his tail hard.

'Off we go!' said Julian, taking the oars. 'Sit over there a bit, Anne. The luggage is weighing down the boat at the other end. Dick, sit by Anne to keep the balance better. That's right. Off we go!'

And off they went in George's boat, rocking up and down on the waves. The sea was fairly calm, but a good breeze blew through their hair. The water splashed around the boat and made a nice gurgly, friendly noise. The children all felt very happy. They were on their own. They were escaping from the horrid Sticks. They were going to stay on Kirrin Island, with the rabbits and gulls and jackdaws.

'Doesn't that new-made bread smell awfully good?' said Dick, feeling very hungry as usual. 'Can we just grab a bit, do you think?'

'Yes, let's,' said George. So they broke off bits of the warm brown crust, handed some to Julian, who was rowing, and chewed the delicious new-made bread. Timmy got a bit too, but his was gone as soon as it went into his mouth.

'Timmy's funny,' said Anne. 'He never eats his food like we do – he seems to *drink* it – just takes it into his mouth and swallows it, as if it was water!'

The others laughed. 'He doesn't drink his bones,' said George. 'He always eats those all right – chews on them for hours and hours. Don't you, Timothy?'

'Woof!' said Timmy, agreeing. He eyed the place where that enormous bone was, wishing he could have it now. But the children wouldn't let him. They were afraid it might go overboard, and that would be a shame.

'I don't think anyone has noticed us going,' said Julian. 'Except Alf, of course. We told him about going to the island, Dick, but nobody else.'

They had called at Alf's house on their way to the cove. Alf was alone in the garden at the back. His mother was away and his father was out fishing. They had told him their secret, and Alf had nodded his tousled head and promised faithfully to tell nobody at all. He was evidently very proud of being trusted.

'If my mum and dad come back, you must let us know,' said George. 'Sail as near the island as you dare, and hail us. You can get nearer to it than anyone else.'

'I'll do that,' promised Alf, wishing he could go with them.

'So, you see, Dick,' said Julian, as he rowed out to the island, 'if by any chance Aunt Fanny does return sooner than we expect, we shall know at once and come back. I think we've planned everything very well.'

'Yes, we have,' said Dick. He turned and faced the island, which was coming nearer. 'We'll soon be there. Isn't George going to take the oars and guide the boat in?'

'Yes,' said George. 'We've come to the difficult bit now, where we've got to weave our way in and out of the different rocks that stick up. Give me the oars, Ju.'

She took the oars, and the others watched in admiration as she guided the big boat skilfully in and out of the hidden rocks. She certainly was very clever. They felt perfectly safe with her.

The boat slid into the little cove. It was a natural harbour, with the water running up to a stretch of sand. High rocks sheltered it. The children jumped out eagerly, and four pairs of willing hands tugged the boat quickly up the sand.

'Higher up still,' panted George. 'You know what awful storms suddenly blow up in this bay. We want to be sure the boat is quite safe, no matter how high the seas run.'

The boat soon lay on one side, high up the stretch of sand. The children sat down, puffing and blowing.

'Let's have breakfast here,' said Julian. 'I don't feel like unloading all those heavy things at the moment. We'll get what we want for breakfast, and have it here on this warm bit of sand.'

They got a loaf of new bread, some cold ham, a few tomatoes and a pot of jam. Anne found knives and forks and plates. Julian opened two bottles of ginger beer.

'Funny sort of breakfast,' he said, setting the bottles down on the sand, 'but absolutely delicious when anyone is as hungry as we are.'

They ate everything except about a third of the loaf. Timmy was given his bone and some of his own biscuits. He crunched up the biscuits at once, and then sat down contentedly to gnaw the wonderful bone.

'How nice to be Timmy – with no plate or knife or fork or cup to bother about,' said Anne, lying on her back in the sun, feeling that she really couldn't eat anything more. 'If we're always going to have mixed-up meals like this on the island, I'll never want to go back. Who would have thought that ham and jam and ginger beer would go so well together?'

Timmy was thirsty. He sat with his tongue hanging out, wishing that George would give him a drink. He didn't like ginger beer.

George eyed him lazily.

'Oh Timmy – are you thirsty?' she said. 'Oh dear, I feel as if I really can't get up! You'll have to wait a few minutes, then I'll go to the boat and empty out some water for you.'

But Timothy couldn't wait. He went off to

some nearby rocks, which were out of reach of the sea. In a hole in one of them he found some rainwater, and he lapped it up eagerly. The children heard him lapping it, and laughed.

'Isn't Timmy clever?' murmured Anne. 'I'd never have thought of that.'

They had been up half the night, and now they were full of good things, and were very sleepy. One by one they fell asleep on the warm sand. Timothy eyed them in astonishment. It wasn't night-time! Yet here were all the children sleeping tightly. Well, a dog could always go to sleep at any time! So Timothy threw himself down beside George, put his head right on her middle, and closed his eyes.

The sun was high when the little group awoke. Julian awoke first, then Dick, feeling very hot indeed, for the sun was blazing down. They sat up, yawning.

'I'm sunburnt!' said Dick, looking at his arms. 'I'll be terribly sore by tonight. Did we bring any cream, Julian?'

'No. We never thought of it,' said Julian. 'Cheer up! We'd better be careful, though. The sun's going to be hot – there's not a cloud in the sky!'

They woke up the girls. George pushed Timmy's head off her tummy.

'You give me nightmares when you put your heavy head there,' she complained. 'Oh, we're on the island, aren't we? For a moment I thought I was back in bed at Kirrin Cottage!'

'Isn't it gorgeous? – here we are for ages, all by ourselves, with tons of nice things to eat, able to do just what we like!' said Anne, contentedly.

'I guess the old Sticks are glad we've gone,' said Dick. 'Spotty Face will be able to loll in the sitting room and read all our books, if he wants to.'

'And Stinker-dog will be able to wander all over the house and lie on anybody's bed without being afraid that Timothy will eat him whole,' said George. 'Well, let him. I don't care about anything now that I've escaped.'

It was fun to lie there and talk about everything. But soon Julian, who could never rest for long once he was awake, got up and stretched himself.

'Come on!' he said to the others. 'There's work to do, Lazy-Bones!'

'Work to do? What do you mean?' said George in astonishment.

'Well, we've got to unload the boat and pack everything somewhere it won't get spoilt if the rain happens to come,' said Julian. 'And we've got to decide exactly where we're going to sleep, and get the heather for our beds and pile the rugs on them. There's lots to do!'

'Oh, don't let's do it yet,' said Anne, not wanting to get up out of the warm sand. But the others pulled her up, and together they all set to work to unload the boat.

'Let's go and have a look at the castle,' said Julian. 'And find the little room where we'll sleep. It's the only one left whole, so it'll have to be that one.'

They went right to the top of the inlet, climbed up onto the rocks and made their way towards the old ruined castle, whose walls rose up from the middle of the little island. They stopped to gaze at it.

'It's a great old ruin,' said Dick. 'Aren't we lucky to have an island and castle of our own! Just think, this is all ours!'

They gazed through a big broken-down archway, to old steps beyond. The castle had once had two fine towers, but now one was almost gone. The other rose high in the air, half-ruined. The black jackdaws collected there, talking loudly. 'Chack, chack, chack! Chack, chack, chack!'

'Nice birds,' said Dick. 'I like them. See the grey patch at the back of their heads, Anne? I wonder if they ever stop talking.'

'I don't think so,' said George. 'Oh, look at the rabbits – tamer than ever!'

The courtyard was full of big rabbits, who eyed them as they came near. It really seemed as if it would be possible to pat them, they were so tame – but one by one they edged away as the children approached.

Timothy was in a great state of excitement, and his tail quivered from end to end. Oh those rabbits! Why couldn't he chase them? Why was George so difficult about rabbits? Why couldn't he make them run a bit?

But George had her hand on his collar, and gave him a stern glance. 'Now, Timothy, don't you *dare* to chase even the smallest of these rabbits. They're mine, every one of them.'

'Ours!' corrected Anne at once. She wanted to share in the rabbits, as well as in the castle and the island.

'Ours!' said George. 'Let's go and have a look at the room where we'll spend the nights.'

They made their way to where the castle didn't seem to be quite so ruined. They came to a doorway and looked inside.

'Here it is!' said Julian, peeping in. 'I'll have to use my torch. The windows are only slits here, and it's quite dark.'

He turned on his torch – and the children all gazed into the old room where they planned to store their goods and sleep.

George gave a loud exclamation. 'We can't use this room! The roof has fallen in since last summer.'

So it had. Julian's torch shone on to a heap of fallen stones, scattered all over the floor. It was impossible to use the old room now. In any case it might be dangerous – it looked as if more stones might fall at any moment.

'Oh no!' said Julian. 'What shall we do about this? We'll have to find somewhere else for a storing and sleeping place!'

# 11 On the old wreck

It was quite a shock to have their plans spoilt. They knew there was no other room in the ruined castle that would shelter them. And they had to find some sort of shelter, because although the weather was fine at the moment, it might rain hard any day – or a storm might blow up.

'And storms around about Kirrin are very violent,' said Julian, remembering one or two. 'Do you remember the storm that tossed your wreck up from the bottom of the sea, George?'

'Oh yes,' said George and Anne, together, and Anne added eagerly: 'Let's go and see the wreck today if we can. I'd love to see if it's still balanced on those rocks, like it was last year, when we explored it.'

'Well, first we have to decide where we're going to sleep,' said Julian, firmly. 'I don't know if you realise it, but it's about three o'clock in the afternoon! We slept for hours on the sand – tired out from our exciting night, I suppose. We really have to find a safe place and put our things there, and make our beds.'

'But where shall we go?' said Dick. 'There's no other place in the old castle.'

'There's the dungeon below,' said Anne, shivering. 'But I don't want to go there. It's so dark and creepy.'

Nobody wanted to sleep down in the dungeons! Dick frowned and thought hard. 'What about the wreck?' he said. 'Any chance of living there?'

'We could go and see,' said Julian. 'I don't fancy living on a damp old rotting wreck – but if it's still high on the rocks, maybe the sun will have dried it, and it might be possible to have our beds and stores there.'

'Let's go and see now,' said George.

They made their way from the ruined castle to the old wall that ran around it. From there they would be able to see the wreck. It had been cast up the year before, and had settled firmly on some rocks.

They stood on the wall and looked for the wreck, but it wasn't where they had expected it to be.

'It's moved,' said Julian, in surprise. 'There it is, look, on those rocks – nearer to the shore than it was before. Poor old wreck! It's been battered about a lot this last winter, hasn't it? It looks much more of a real wreck than it did last summer.'

'I don't think we'll be able to sleep there,' said Dick. 'It's badly battered. We might be able to store food there, though. You know, I think we could get to it from those rocks that run out from the island!'

'Yes, I think we could,' said George. 'We could only reach it safely by boat last summer – but when the tide is down, I think we *could* climb out over the line of rocks, right to the wreck itself.'

'We'll try in about an hour,' said Julian, feeling excited. 'The tide will be off the rocks by then.'

'Let's go and have a look at the old well,' said Dick, and they made their way back to the courtyard of the castle.

Here, the summer before, they had found the entrance to the well-shaft that ran deep down through the rock, past the dungeons below, lower than the level of the sea, to fresh water.

The children looked about for the well, and came to the old wooden cover. They drew it back.

'There are the rungs of the old iron ladder I went down last year,' said Dick, peering in. 'Now let's find the entrance to the dungeon. The steps down into it are somewhere near here.'

They found the entrance, but to their surprise some enormous stones had been pulled across it.

'Who did that?' said George, frowning. 'We didn't. Someone has been here!'

'Tourists, I suppose,' said Julian. 'Remember that we thought we saw a spire of smoke here the other day? I bet it was tourists. You know, the story of Kirrin Island, and its old castle and dungeons, and the treasure we found in it last year, was in all the newspapers. I expect one of the fishermen has been making money by taking tourists and landing them on *our* island.'

'How dare they?' said George, looking very fierce. 'I'll put up a board that says "Trespassers will be sent to prison". I won't have strangers on our island.'

'Well, don't worry about the stones pulled across the dungeon entrance,' said Julian. 'I don't think any of us wants to go down there. Look at poor old Timmy staring at those rabbits and looking miserable! Isn't he funny?'

Timothy was sitting down behind the children, looking most mournfully at the ring of rabbits all around the weed-grown courtyard. He looked at the rabbits and then he looked at George, then he looked back at the rabbits.

'No good, Timmy,' said George, firmly. 'I'm not going to change my mind about rabbits. You're not to chase them on our island.'

'I expect he thinks you're very unfair to him,' said Anne. 'After all, you said he might share your quarter of the island with you – and so he thinks he ought to have his share of your rabbits too!'

Everyone laughed. Timmy wagged his tail and looked hopefully at George. They all walked across the courtyard – and then Julian suddenly came to a stop.

'Look!' he said in surprise, pointing to something on the ground. 'Look! Someone *has* been here! This is where they built a fire!'

Everyone gazed at the ground. There was a heap of wood-ash there, evidently left from a fire. Stamped into the ground was a cigarette end, too. There was absolutely no doubt about it – someone had been on the island!

'If tourists come here I'll set Timmy on to them!' cried George, in a fury. 'This is our place, it doesn't belong to anybody else at all. Timothy, you mustn't chase rabbits here, but you can chase anybody on two legs, except us! See?'

Timmy wagged his tail at once. 'Woof!' he said, quite agreeing. He looked all around as if he hoped to see somebody appearing that he could chase. But there was no one.

'I should think the tide is about off those rocks by now,' said Julian. 'Let's go and see. If it is we'll climb along them and see if we can get to the wreck. Anne had better not come. She might slip and fall, and the sea is raging all around the rocks.'

'Of course I'm coming!' cried Anne, indignantly. 'You're just as likely to fall as I am.'

'Well, I'll see if it looks too dangerous,' said Julian.

They made their way over the castle wall, down to the line of rocks that ran out seawards, towards the wreck. Big waves did wash over the rocks occasionally, but it seemed fairly safe.

'If you keep between me and Dick, you can

come, Anne,' said Julian. 'But you must let us help you over difficult parts, and not make a fuss. We don't want you to fall in and get washed away.'

They began to make their way along the line of rugged, slippery rocks. The tide went down even farther as they got nearer to the wreck, and soon there was very little danger of being washed off the rocks. It was possible now to get right to the wreck across the rocks – something they had not been able to do the summer before.

'Here we are!' said Julian at last, and he put his hand on the side of the old wreck. She was a big ship now that they were near to her. She towered above them, thick with shellfish and seaweed, smelling musty and old. The water washed around the bottom part of her, but the top part was right out of the water, even when the tide was at its highest.

'She was thrown about a bit last winter,' said George, looking at her. 'There are a lot more new holes in her side, aren't there? And part of her old mast is gone, and some of the deck. How can we get up to her?'

'I've got a rope,' said Julian, and he undid a

rope that he had wound around his waist. 'Just a minute – I'll make a loop and see if I can throw it around that post sticking out up there.'

He threw the rope two or three times, but couldn't get the loop around the post. George took it from him impatiently. At the first throw she got it around the post. She was very good indeed at things like that, Anne thought admiringly.

She was up the rope like a monkey, and soon stood on the sloping slippery deck. She almost slipped, but caught at a broken piece of deck just in time. Julian helped Anne to go up, and then the two boys followed.

'It's a horrible smell, isn't it?' said Anne, wrinkling up her nose. 'Do all wrecks smell like this? I don't think I'll go and look down in the cabins like we did last time. The smell would be worse there.'

So the others left Anne up on the half-rotten deck while they went to explore. They went down to the smelly, seaweed-hung cabins, and into the captain's old cabin, the biggest of the lot. But it was obvious that not only could they not sleep there, but they couldn't store anything there, either. The whole place was damp and rotten.

Julian was half afraid his foot would go through the planking at any moment.

'Let's go up to the deck,' he said. 'It's nasty down here – really dark too.'

They were just going up, when they heard a shout from Anne. 'Come here, quick! I've found something!'

They hurried up as fast as they could, slipping and sliding on the sloping deck. Anne was standing where they had left her, her eyes shining brightly. She was pointing to something on the opposite side of the ship.

'What is it?' said George. 'What's the matter?'

'Look – that wasn't here when we came here before, surely!' said Anne, still pointing. The others looked where she pointed. They saw an open locker at the other side of the deck, and stuffed into it was a small black trunk! How extraordinary!

'A little black trunk!' said Julian, in surprise. 'No – that wasn't there before. It's not been there long either – it's quite dry and new! Whoever does it belong to? And why should it be here?'

## 12  The cave in the cliff

Cautiously the children made their way down the slippery deck towards the locker. The door of this had evidently been shut on the trunk but had come open, so that the trunk wasn't hidden, as had been intended.

Julian pulled out the little black trunk. All the children were amazed. *Why* should anyone put a trunk there?

'Smugglers, do you think?' said Dick, his eyes gleaming.

'It might be,' said Julian, thoughtfully, trying to undo the straps of the trunk. 'This would be a very good place for smugglers. Ships that knew the way could put in, cast off a boat with smuggled goods, leave them here, and go on their way, knowing that people could come and collect the goods another time.'

'Do you think there are smuggled goods inside the trunk?' asked Anne, in excitement. 'What would there be? Diamonds?'

'Anything that has tax to be paid on it before it can get into the country,' said Julian. 'Bother these straps! I can't undo them.'

'Let *me* try,' said Anne, who had very deft little fingers. She began to work at the buckles, and in a short time had the straps undone. But a further disappointment awaited them. The trunk was well and truly locked! There were two good locks, and no keys!

'How annoying!' said George. 'How can we get the trunk open now?'

'We can't,' said Julian. 'And we mustn't smash it open, because that would warn whoever it belongs to that the goods had been found. We don't want to warn the smugglers that we've discovered their little game. We want to try to catch them!'

'Ooooh!' said Anne, going red with excitement. 'Catch the smugglers! Oh Julian! Do you really think we could?'

'Why not?' said Julian. 'No one knows we're here. If we hid whenever we saw a ship approaching the island, we might see a boat coming to it, and we could watch and find out what's happening. I should think that the smugglers are using this island as a sort of dropping-place for goods. I wonder who comes and fetches them? Someone from Kirrin village or the nearby places, I should think.'

'This is going to be so exciting,' said Dick. 'We always seem to have adventures when we come to Kirrin. It's absolutely *full* of them. This will be the third one we've had.'

'I think we ought to be getting back over the rocks,' said Julian, suddenly looking over the side of the ship and seeing that the tide had turned. 'Come on – we don't want to be caught by the tide and have to stay here for hours and hours! I'll go down the rope first. Then you come, Anne.'

They were soon climbing over the rocks again, feeling very excited. Just as they reached the last stretch of rocks leading to the rocky cliff of the island itself, Dick stopped.

'What's up?' said George, pushing behind him. 'Go on!'

'Isn't that a cave, just past that big rock there?' said Dick, pointing. 'It looks like one to me. If it is, it'd be a great place to store our things in, and even to sleep in, if it's out of reach of the sea.'

'There aren't any caves on Kirrin,' began George, and then she stopped short. What Dick was pointing at really did look like a cave. It was worth checking. After all, George had never explored this line of rocks, and so had never been able to catch sight of the cave. It couldn't possibly be seen from the land.

'We'll go and see,' she said. So they changed their direction, and instead of climbing back the way they had come, they cut across the mass of rock and made their way towards a jutting-out part of the cliff, in which the cave seemed to be.

They came to it at last. Steep rocks guarded the entrance, and half hid it. Except from where Dick had seen it, it was really impossible to catch sight of it, it was so well hidden.

'It *is* a cave!' said Dick, in delight, stepping into it. 'And it's a great one!'

It really was ideal. Its floor was spread with fine white sand, as soft as powder, and perfectly dry, for the cave was clearly higher than the tide reached, except, possibly, in a bad winter storm. Around one side of it ran a stone ledge.

'Exactly like a shelf made for us!' cried Anne.

'We can put all our things here. How lovely! Let's come and live here and sleep here. And look, Julian, we've even got a skylight in the roof!'

The little girl pointed upwards, and the others saw that the roof of the cave was open in one part, going out to the cliff-top. It was plain that somewhere on the heathery cliff above was a hole that looked down to the cave, making what Anne called a 'skylight'.

'We could drop all our things down through that hole,' said Julian, quickly making plans. 'It would take ages to bring them over the rocks. If we can find that hole up there when we're out on the cliff again, we can let down everything on a rope. It's not a very high "skylight", as Anne calls it – the cliffs are low just here. I think we could swing ourselves down a rope easily, so we needn't have the bother of clambering over the rocks to the sea entrance!'

This was an amazing discovery. 'Our island is even more exciting than we thought,' said Anne, happily. 'We've got a beautiful cave to share now!'

The next thing to do, of course, was to go up on the cliff and find the hole that led to the roof of the cave. So out they all went, Timmy too.

Timmy was funny on the slippery rocks. His feet slithered about, and two or three times he fell into the water. But he just swam across the pools he fell into, clambered out and went on again with his slithering.

'He's like George!' said Anne, with a laugh. 'He never gives up, whatever happens to him!'

They climbed up to the top of the cliff. It was easy to find the hole once they knew it was there.

'Pretty dangerous, really,' said Julian, when he had found it, and was peering down. 'Any one of us might have run on this cliff and popped down the hole by accident. See, it's all criss-crossed with blackberry brambles.'

They scratched their hands, trying to free the hole from the brambles. Once they had cleared the hole, they could look right down into the cave quite easily.

'It's not very far down,' said Anne. 'It looks almost as if we could jump down, if we let ourselves slide down this hole.'

'Don't you do anything of the sort,' said Julian. 'You'd break your leg. Wait till we get a rope fixed up, hanging down into the cave. Then we can manage to get in and out easily.'

They went back to the boat, and began unloading it. They took everything across to the seaward side of the island, where the cave was. Julian took a strong rope and knotted it thickly at intervals.

'To give our feet a hold as we go down,' he explained. 'If we drop down too quickly, we'll hurt our hands. These knots will stop us slipping and help us to climb up.'

'Let me go down first, and then you can lower all our things to me,' said George.

So down she went, hand over hand, her feet easily finding the thick knots, feeling for one after another. It was a good way to go down.

'How will we get Timmy down?' said Julian. But Timothy, who had been whining anxiously at the edge of the hole, watching George sliding away from him, solved the difficulty himself.

He jumped into the hole and disappeared down it! There came a shriek from below.

'Oh! What's this? Oh *Timmy*! Have you hurt yourself?'

The sand was very soft, like a velvet cushion, and Tim had not hurt himself at all. He gave himself a shake and then barked joyfully. He was with George again! He wasn't going to have his mistress disappearing down mysterious holes without following her at once. Not Timmy!

Then followed the business of lowering down all the goods. Anne and Dick tied the things together in rugs, and Julian lowered them carefully. George untied the rope as soon as it reached her, took out the goods, and then back went the rope again to be tied around another bundle.

'Last one!' called Julian, after a long time of really hard work. 'Then down we come too, and before we make our beds or anything, our next job is to have a good meal! It's hours and hours since we had a meal, and I'm starving.'

Soon they were all sitting on the warm, soft floor of the cave. They opened a tin of meat, cut huge slices of bread and made sandwiches. Then they opened a tin of pineapple chunks and ate those, spooning them out of the tin, full of sweetness and juice. After that they still felt hungry, so they opened two tins of sardines and dug them out with biscuits. It made a really delicious meal.

'Ginger beer to finish up with, please,' said Dick. 'Why don't people always have meals like this?'

'We'd better hurry up or we won't be able to get heather for our beds,' said George, sleepily.

'Who wants heather?' said Dick. '*I* don't! This lovely soft sand is all *I'll* want – and a cushion and a rug or two. I'll sleep better here than ever I did in bed!'

So the rugs and cushions were spread out on the sandy floor of the cave. A candle was lit as it grew dark, and the four sleepy children looked at one another. Timmy, as usual, was with George.

'Goodnight,' said George. 'I can't keep awake another minute. Goodnight, ev . . . ery . . . body . . . good . . . night!

## 13 A day on the island

The children hardly knew where they were the next day when they woke up. The sun was pouring into the cave entrance, and fell first of all on George's sleeping face. It awoke her and she lay half dozing, wondering why her bed felt less soft than usual.

'But I'm not in my bed – I'm on Kirrin Island, of course!' she thought suddenly to herself. She sat up and gave Anne a punch. 'Wake up, sleepyhead! We're on the island!'

Soon they were all awake, rubbing the sleep from their eyes.

'I think I'm going to get heather today for my bed, after all,' said Anne. 'The sand feels soft at first, but it gets hard after a bit.'

The others agreed that they would all get heather and lay it on the sand, with rugs for covering. Then they would have really fine beds.

'It's fun to live in a cave,' said Dick. 'Isn't it

amazing having a fine cave like this on our island, as well as a castle and dungeons! We're so lucky.'

'I feel sticky and dirty,' said Julian. 'Let's go and have a swim before we have breakfast. Then cold ham, bread, pickles and marmalade for me!'

'We'll be cold after our swim,' said George. 'We'd better light my little stove and put the kettle on to boil while we're swimming. Then we can make some hot cocoa when we come back shivering!'

'Oh yes,' said Anne, who had never boiled anything on such a tiny stove before. 'I'll fill the kettle with water from one of the containers. What shall we do for milk?'

'There's a tin of milk somewhere in the pile,' said Julian. 'We can open that. Where's the tin opener?'

They couldn't find it, which was very exasperating. But at last Julian discovered it in his pocket.

The little stove was filled with methylated spirit, and lit. The kettle was filled and set on top. Then the children went off for a swim.

'Look! There's a pool in the middle of those

rocks over there!' called Julian, pointing. 'We've never spotted it before. It's like a small swimming pool, especially for us!'

'Kirrin Swimming Pool, twenty pence a dip!' said Dick. 'Free to the owners, though! Come on – it looks gorgeous! And see how the waves keep washing over the top of the rocks and splashing into the pool. Couldn't be better!'

It was a lovely rock pool, deep, clear and not too cold. They all enjoyed themselves thoroughly, splashing about and swimming and floating. George tried a dive off one of the rocks, and went in beautifully.

'George can do anything in the water,' said Anne, admiringly. 'I wish I could dive and swim like her.'

'We can see the old wreck nicely from here,' said Julian, coming out of the water. 'Oh no! We didn't bring any towels.'

'We'll use one of the rugs, turn and turn about,' said Dick. 'I'll go and fetch the thinnest one. Hey – do you remember that trunk we saw in the wreck yesterday? Strange, wasn't it?'

'Yes, very strange,' said Julian. 'I don't understand it. We'll have to keep a watch on the wreck and see who comes to collect the trunk.'

'I suppose the smugglers – if they are smugglers – will come slinking around this side of the island and quietly send off a boat to the wreck,' said George, drying herself vigorously. 'Well, we'd better keep a strict look-out, and see if anything appears on the sea out there.'

'Yes. We don't want them to spot us,' said Dick. 'We won't find out anything if they see us and are warned. They'd give up coming to the island. I vote we each take turns at keeping a look-out, so that we can spot anything at once and get under cover.'

'Good idea!' said Julian. 'Well, I'm dry, but not very warm. Let's race to the cave, and get that hot drink. And breakfast – I could eat a whole chicken and probably a duck as well, not to mention a turkey.'

The others laughed. They all felt the same. They raced off to the cave, running over the sand and climbing over a few rocks, then down to the cave-beach and into the big entrance, still splashed with sunshine.

The kettle was boiling away merrily, sending a cloud of steam up from its tin spout.

'Get the ham out and a loaf of bread, and that jar of pickles we brought,' said Julian. 'I'll open the tin of milk. George, you take the tin of cocoa and that jug, and make enough for all of us.'

'I'm so happy,' said Anne, as she sat at the entrance to the cave, eating her breakfast. 'It's a lovely feeling. It's wonderful being on our island like this, all by ourselves, able to do what we like.'

They all felt the same. It was such a lovely day too, and the sky and sea were so blue. They sat eating and drinking, gazing out to sea, watching the waves break into spray over the rocks beyond the old wreck. It certainly was a very rocky coast.

'Let's arrange everything very nicely in the cave,' said Anne, who was the tidiest of the four. 'This will be our home. We'll make four proper beds. And we'll each have our own place to sit in. And we'll arrange everything tidily on that big stone shelf there. It might have been made for us!'

'Let's leave Anne to play houses by herself,' said George, who was longing to stretch her legs again. 'We'll go and get some heather for beds.

Oh! – what about one of us keeping a watch on the old wreck, to see if anyone comes?'

'Yes – that's important,' said Julian at once. 'I'll take first watch. The best place would be up on the cliff just above this cave. I can find a gorse bush that'll hide me from anyone out at sea. You two get the heather. We'll take two-hourly watches. We can read if we like, as long as we keep on looking up.'

Dick and George went to get the heather. Julian climbed up the knotted rope that hung down through the hole, tied firmly to the great old root of an enormous gorse bush. He pulled himself out on the cliff and lay on the heather, panting.

He could see nothing out at sea at all except for a big tanker miles out on the skyline. He lay down in the sun, enjoying the warmth that poured onto every inch of his body. This look-out job was going to be very nice!

He could hear Anne singing down in the cave as she tidied up her 'house'. Her voice came up through the cave roof hole, rather muffled. Julian smiled. He knew Anne was really enjoying herself.

So she was. She had washed the few bits of

crockery they had used for breakfast, in a convenient little rain-pool outside the cave. Timmy used it for drinking water too, but he didn't seem to mind Anne using it for washing-up water, though she apologised to him for doing so.

'I'm sorry if I spoil your drinking water, Timmy darling,' she said, 'but you're such a sensible dog that I know if it suddenly tastes nasty to you, you'll go off and find another rain-pool.'

'Woof!' said Timmy, and ran off to meet George, who was just arriving back with Dick, armed with masses of soft, sweet-smelling heather for beds.

'Put the heather outside the cave, please, George', said Anne. 'I'll make the beds inside when I'm ready.'

'Right!' said George. 'We'll go and get some more. Isn't this fun?'

'Julian's gone up the rope to the top of the cliff,' said Anne. 'He'll yell if he sees anything unusual. I hope he does, don't you?'

'It would be exciting,' agreed Dick, putting down his heather on top of Timmy, and nearly burying him. 'Oh sorry, Timmy – are you there? Bad luck!'

Anne had a very happy morning. She arranged everything neatly on the shelf – crockery and knives and forks and spoons in one place – saucepan and kettle in another – tins of meat next, tins of soup together, tins of fruit neatly piled on top of one another. It was a very tidy kitchen shelf!

She wrapped all the bread up in an old tablecloth they had brought, and put it at the back of the cave in the coolest place she could find. The containers of water went there too, and so did all the bottles of drinks.

Then Anne set to work to make the beds. She decided to make two nice big ones, one on each side of the cave.

'George and I and Tim will have the one this side,' she thought, patting down the heather into the shape of a bed. 'And Julian and Dick can have the other side. I'll need lots more heather. Oh, is that you, Dick? You're just in time! I need more heather.'

Soon the beds were made, and each had an old rug for an under-blanket, and two better rugs for covers. Cushions made pillows.

'What a pity we didn't bring night-things,'

thought Anne. 'I could have folded them neatly and put them under the cushions. There! It all looks lovely. We've got a beautiful house.'

Julian came sliding down the rope from the cliff to the cave. He looked around admiringly. 'Anne, the cave looks great! Everything in order and looking so tidy. You've done really well.'

Anne was pleased to hear Julian's praise.

'Yes, it does look nice, doesn't it?' she said. 'But why aren't you watching up on the cliff, Ju?'

'It's Dick's turn now,' said Julian. 'The two hours are up. Did we bring any biscuits? I feel as if I could do with one or two, and I bet the others could too. Let's all go up to the cliff-top and have some. George and Timmy are there with Dick.'

Anne knew exactly where to put her hand on the tin of biscuits. She took out ten and climbed up to the cliff-top. Julian went up the rope. Soon all five were sitting by the big gorse bush, nibbling at biscuits, Timmy too. At least, he didn't nibble. He just swallowed.

The day passed very happily and rather lazily. They took turns at being look-out, though Anne was told off by Julian in the afternoon for falling asleep during her watch. She was very ashamed of herself and cried.

'You're too little to be a look-out, that's what it is,' said Julian. 'We three and Timmy had better do it.'

'Oh, no, please let me too,' begged poor Anne. 'I never, never will fall asleep again. But the sun was so hot and . . .'

'Don't make excuses,' said Julian. 'It only makes things worse if you do. All right – we'll give you another chance, Anne, and see if you're really big enough to do the things we do.'

But though they all took their turns, and kept a watch for any strange vessel, none appeared. The children were disappointed. They longed to know who had put that trunk on the wreck and why, and what it contained.

'Better go to bed now,' said Julian, when the sun sank low. 'It's about nine o'clock. Come on! I'm really looking forward to a sleep on those lovely heathery beds that Anne has made!'

## 14 Disturbance in the night

It was dark in the cave, not really quite dark enough to light a candle, but the cave looked so nice by candlelight that it was fun to light one. So Anne took the matches and lit a candle. At once strange shadows jumped all around the cave, and it became a rather exciting place, not at all like the cave they knew by daylight!

'I wish we could have a fire,' said Anne.

'We'd be far too hot,' said Julian. 'And it would smoke us out. You can't have a fire in a cave like this. There's no chimney.'

'Yes, there is,' said Anne, pointing to the hole in the roof. 'If we lit a fire just under that hole, it would act as a chimney, wouldn't it?'

'It might,' said Dick, thoughtfully. 'But I don't think so. We'd just get the cave full of stifling smoke, and we wouldn't be able to sleep for choking.'

'Well, couldn't we light a fire at the cave entrance then?' said Anne who felt that a real home ought to have a fire somewhere. 'Just to keep away wild beasts, say! That's what cavemen did hundreds of years ago. They lit fires at the cave entrance at night to keep away any wild animal that might be prowling around.'

'Well, what wild beasts do you think are likely to come and peep into this cave?' asked Julian, lazily, finishing a cup of cocoa. 'Lions? Tigers? Or perhaps you're afraid of an elephant or two.'

Everyone laughed. 'No – I don't really think animals like that would come,' said Anne. 'Only – it would be nice to have a red, glowing fire to watch when we go to sleep.'

'Perhaps Anne thinks the rabbits might come in and nibble our toes or something,' said Dick.

'Woof!' said Tim, pricking up his ears as he always did at the mention of rabbits.

'I don't think we ought to have a fire,' said Julian, 'because it might be seen out at sea and give a warning to anyone thinking of coming to the island to do a bit of smuggling.'

'No, Julian – the entrance to this cave is so well hidden that I'm sure no one could see a fire out at sea,' said George, at once. 'There's that line of high rocks in front, which must hide it completely.

I think it'd be fun to have a fire. It'd light up the cave so strangely and excitingly.'

'Oh good, George!' said Anne, delighted to find someone agreeing with her.

'Well, we can't trek out and get sticks for it now,' said Dick, who was far too comfortable to move.

'You don't need to,' said Anne, eagerly. 'I got lots myself today, and stored them at the back of the cave, in case we wanted a fire.'

'Isn't she a good housekeeper!' said Julian, in great admiration. 'She may go to sleep when she's look-out, but she's wide awake enough when it comes to making a house for us out of a cave! All right, Anne – we'll make a fire for you!'

They all got up and fetched the sticks from the back of the cave. Anne had been to the jackdaw tower and had picked up armfuls that the birds had dropped when making their nests in the tower. They built them up to make a nice little fire. Julian got some dried seaweed too, to drop into it.

They lit the fire at the cave entrance, and the dry sticks blazed up at once. The children went back to their heather beds, and lay down on them, watching the red flames leaping and crackling. The red glow lit up the cave and made it very strange and exciting.

'This is lovely,' said Anne, half asleep. 'Really lovely. Oh Timmy, move a bit. You're so heavy on my feet. Here, George, pull Timothy over to your side. You're used to him lying on you.'

'Goodnight,' said Dick, sleepily. 'The fire is dying down, but I can't be bothered to put any more wood on it. I'm sure all the lions and tigers and bears and elephants have been frightened away.'

'Silly!' said Anne. 'You needn't tease me about it – you've enjoyed it as much as I have! Goodnight.'

They all fell asleep and dreamed peacefully of many things. Julian awoke with a jump. Some strange noise had awakened him. He lay still, listening.

Timothy was growling deeply, right down in his throat. 'R-r-r-r-r-r-r,' he went. 'Gr-r-r-r-r-r-r-r!'

George awoke too, and put out her hand sleepily. 'What's the matter, Tim?' she said.

'He's heard something, George,' said Julian, in a low voice from his bed on the other side of the cave.

George sat up cautiously. Timmy was still growling. 'Sh!' said George and he stopped. He was sitting up straight, his ears well cocked.

'Perhaps it's the smugglers come in the night,' whispered George, and a funny prickly feeling ran down her back. Somehow smugglers in the daytime were exciting and quite welcome – but at night they seemed different. George didn't want to meet any just then!

'I'm going out to see if I can spot anything,' said Julian, getting off his bed quietly, so as not to wake Dick. 'I'll go up the rope to the top of the cliff. I can see better from there.'

'Take my torch,' said George. But Julian didn't want it.

'No, thanks. I can feel the way up that knotted rope quite well, whether I can see or not,' he said.

He went up the rope in the dark, his body twisting around as the rope turned. He climbed up onto the cliff and looked out to sea. It was a very dark night, and he could see no ship at all, not even the wreck. It was far too dark.

'Pity there's no moon,' thought Julian. 'I might be able to see something then.'

He watched for a few minutes, and then George's voice came through the hole in the roof, coming out strangely at his feet.

'Julian! Is there anything to see? Shall I come up?'

'Nothing at all,' said Julian. 'Is Timmy still growling?'

'Yes, when I take my hand off his collar,' said George. 'I can't think what's upset him.'

Suddenly Julian caught sight of something. It was a light, a good way beyond the line of rocks. He watched in excitement. That would be just about where the wreck was! Yes – it must be someone on the wreck with a lantern!

'George! Come up!' he said, putting his head inside the hole.

George came up, hand over hand, like a monkey, leaving Timothy growling below. She sat by Julian on the cliff-top.

'See the wreck – look, over there!' said Julian. 'At least, you can't see the wreck itself, it's too dark – but you can see a lantern that someone has put there.'

'Yes – that's someone on our wreck, with a lantern!' said George, feeling excited. 'Oh, I wonder if it's the smugglers – coming to bring more things.'

'Or somebody fetching that trunk,' said Julian. 'Well, we'll know tomorrow, for we'll go and see. Look! – whoever is there is moving off now – the light of the lantern is going lower – they must be getting into a boat by the side of the wreck. And now the light's gone out.'

The children strained their ears to try to hear the splash of oars or the sound of voices over the water. They both thought they could hear voices.

'The boat must have gone off to join a ship or something,' said Julian. 'I think I can see a faint light right out there – out at sea, look! Maybe the boat is going to it.'

There was nothing more to see or hear, and soon the two of them slid down the knotted rope back to the cave. They didn't wake the others, who were still sleeping peacefully. Timothy leapt up and licked Julian and George, whining joyfully. He didn't growl any more.

'You're a good dog, aren't you?' said Julian, patting him. 'Nothing ever escapes your sharp ears, does it?'

Timothy settled down on George's feet again. It

was plain that whatever it was that had disturbed him had gone. It must have been the presence of the stranger or strangers on the old wreck. Well, they would go there in the morning and see if they could discover what had been taken away or brought there in the night.

Anne and Dick were most indignant the next morning when they heard Julian's tale.

'You *might* have woken us!' said Dick, crossly.

'We would have if there had been anything much to see,' said George. 'But there was just the light from a lantern, and nothing else except that we thought we heard the sound of voices.'

When the tide was low enough the children and Timothy set off over the rocks to the wreck. They clambered up and stood on the slanting, slippery deck. They looked towards the locker where the little trunk had stood. The door of the locker was shut this time.

Julian slid down towards it and tried to pull it open. Someone had stuffed a piece of wood in to keep the locker from swinging open. Julian pulled it out. Then the door opened easily.

'Anything else in there?' said George, stepping carefully over the slimy deck to Julian.

'Yes,' said Julian. 'Look! Tins of food! And cups and plates and things – just as if someone was going to come and live on the island too! Isn't it funny? The trunk is still here too, locked as before. And here are some candles – and a little lamp – and a bundle of rags. Whatever *are* they here for?'

It really was a puzzle. Julian frowned for a few minutes, trying to think it out.

'It looks as if someone's going to come and stay on the island for a bit – probably to wait here and take in whatever goods are going to be smuggled. Well – we'll be on the look-out for them, day or night!'

They left the wreck, feeling excited. They had a good hiding place in their cave – no one could possibly find them there. And, from their hiding place, they could watch anyone coming to and from the wreck, and from the wreck to the island.

'What about our cove, where we put our boat?' said George, suddenly. 'They might use that cove, you know – if they came in a boat. It's dangerous to reach the island from the wreck, if anyone tried to get to the rocky beach nearby.'

'Well – if anyone came to our cove, they'd see

our boat,' said Dick, in alarm. 'We'd better hide it, hadn't we?'

'How?' said Anne, thinking that it would be a difficult thing to hide a boat as big as theirs.

'Don't know,' said Julian. 'We'll go and have a look.'

All four and Timmy went off to the cove into which they had rowed their boat. The boat was pulled high up, out of reach of the waves. George explored the cove well, and then had an idea.

'Do you think we could pull the boat around this big rock? It would just about hide it, though anyone going around the rock would see it at once.'

The others thought it would be worth trying, anyway. So, with much panting and puffing, they hauled the boat around the rock, which almost completely hid her.

'Good!' said George, going down into the cove to see if very much of the boat showed. 'A bit of her does show still. Let's drape it with seaweed!'

So they draped the prow of the boat with all the seaweed they could find, and after that, unless anyone went deliberately around the big rock, the boat really wasn't noticeable at all.

'Good!' said Julian, looking at his watch. 'Hey
– it's long past tea-time – and, you know, while
we've been doing all this with the boat, we forgot
to have someone on the look-out post on the cliff-
top. What idiots we are!'

'Well, I don't expect anything has happened
since we've been away from the cave,' said Dick,
putting a fine big bit of seaweed on the prow of
the boat, as a last touch. 'I bet the smugglers will
only come at night.'

'I expect you're right,' said Julian. 'I think
we'd better keep a look-out at night, too. The
look-out could take rugs up to the cliff-top and
curl up there.'

'Timmy could be with whoever is keeping
watch,' said Anne. 'Then if the look-out goes to
sleep by mistake, Timmy would growl and wake
them up if he saw anything.'

'You mean, when *you* go to sleep,' said Dick,
grinning. 'Come on – let's get back to the cave
and have some tea.'

And then Timothy suddenly began to
growl again!

## 15  Who is on the island?

'Shh!' said Julian, at once. 'Get down behind this bush, quick, everyone!'

They had left the cove and were walking towards the castle when Timmy growled. Now they all crouched behind a mass of brambles, their hearts beating fast.

'Don't growl, Timmy,' said George, in Timothy's nearest ear. He stopped at once, but he stood stiff and quivering, on the watch.

Julian peeped through the bush, parting the brambles and scratching his hands. He could just see somebody in the courtyard – one person – two persons – maybe three. He strained his eyes to try to see, but as he looked, they disappeared.

'I think they've moved those big stones over the entrance to the dungeons, and have gone down there,' he whispered. 'Stay here, and I'll creep out a bit and see. I won't let anyone spot me.'

He came back and nodded. 'Yes – they've gone

down the dungeons. Do you think they can be the smugglers? Do you suppose they're storing their smuggled goods down there? It would be a perfect place, of course.'

'Let's get back to the cave while they are underground,' said George. 'I'm worried Timmy will give the game away by barking. He's just bursting himself trying not to make some sort of noise.'

'Come on, then!' said Julian. 'Don't go across the courtyard – make for the shore and we'll scramble around it till we get to the cave. Then one of us can pop up through the hole and hide behind that big gorse bush there to see who the smugglers are. They must have come in by boat either from the wreck, or by rowing cleverly through the rocks off-shore.'

They got to the cave at last and went in. But no sooner had Julian shinned up the rope, helped by the others, than Timothy disappeared! He ran out of the cave while the others' backs were turned, and when George turned around there was no Timmy to be seen!

'Timmy!' she called in a low voice. 'Timmy! Where are you?'

But no answer came! Timmy had gone off on his own. If only the smugglers didn't see him! What a bad dog he was to do that!

But Timmy had smelt something exciting – he had smelt a smell he knew – a dog-smell – and he meant to find the owner of it and bite off his ears and tail! 'Gr-r-r-r-r!' Timmy wasn't going to allow dogs on *his* island!

Julian sat close beside the gorse bush, watching all around. There was nothing to be seen on the wreck, and there was no ship out to sea. Probably the boat that had brought the strangers to the island was hidden down below among the rocks. Julian looked behind him, towards the castle – and as he looked, he saw an astonishing sight!

A dog was sniffing at the bushes not far away – and creeping up behind him, all his hackles up, was Timothy! Timothy was stalking the dog as if he were a cat stalking a rabbit! The other dog suddenly heard him and leapt around, facing Timothy. Timmy flung himself on the dog with a blood-curdling howl, and the dog howled in fright.

Julian watched in horror, not knowing what to do. The two dogs made a fearful noise, especially the other dog, whose howls of terror and yelps of rage resounded everywhere.

'This will bring the smugglers up, and they'll see Timmy and know there's someone on the island,' thought Julian. 'Oh Timmy! – why didn't you stay with George and keep quiet?'

From the walls of the ruined castle came three figures, running to see what was happening to their dog – and Julian stared at them in amazement – for the three people were Mr Stick, Mrs Stick and Edgar!

'They've come after us!' said Julian, crawling around the bush to get to the hole quickly. 'They've guessed we're here and they've come to look for us, to make us go back! Well, they won't find us! What a pity Timmy's given us away!'

There came a shrill whistle from down below him. It was George, who, hearing the row from the dogs, was feeling worried, and had sent out her piercing whistle for Timmy. It was a whistle the dog always obeyed, and he let go of the dog and shot off to the cliff-top at once, just as the three Sticks arrived on the scene, and picked up their bleeding, whining mongrel.

Edgar tore after Timmy, up to the cliff-top.

Julian dropped down to the cave when he spotted Edgar approaching. Timmy ran to the hole and dropped bodily down, landing almost on top of Julian. He flung himself on George.

'Shut up, shut up!' said George, in an urgent whisper to the excited dog. 'Do you want to give our hiding place away, you idiot?'

Edgar, panting and puffing, arrived on the cliff-top, and was completely amazed to see Timothy apparently disappear into the solid earth. He hunted about for a bit, but it was clear that the dog was no longer on the cliff.

Mr and Mrs Stick came up too.

'Where did that dog go?' shouted Mrs Stick. 'What was he like?'

'He looked like that horrible dog of the children's,' said Edgar. His voice could clearly be heard by everyone down in the cave. The children kept as quiet as mice.

'But it *couldn't* be!' came Mrs Stick's voice. 'The children have gone home – we saw them, *and* the dog too, making off towards the railway. It must be some sort of stray dog left here by a tourist.'

'Well, where is he, then?' said Mr Stick's hoarse

voice. 'Can't see any dog anywhere about now.'

'He disappeared into the earth,' said Edgar, in a surprised voice.

Mr Stick made a rude and scornful noise. 'You tell lovely tales, you do,' he said. 'Disappeared into the earth! What next? Fell over the cliff, I should think. Well, he got his teeth into poor Tinker good and proper. If I see that dog, I'll shoot him!'

'He might have some hiding place on this cliff,' said Mrs Stick. 'Let's have a look!'

The children sat as quiet as mice, George with a warning hand on Timmy's collar. They could hear that the Sticks were really very near. Julian expected one of them to fall down the hole at any moment!

But mercifully they didn't find the hole that led down to the cave. They stood quite near to it, though, while they were discussing the problem.

'If it's the children's dog, then those tiresome kids must have come to this island, instead of going home,' said Mrs Stick. 'That would ruin our plan! We'll have to find out. I'll have no peace till I know.'

'We can soon find out,' said Mr Stick. 'No need

to worry about that. Their boat will be here somewhere – and they'll all be about, too! It's impossible for four children, a dog and a boat to be hidden on this small island once anyone starts hunting for them! Edgar, you go around that way. Clara, you go around the castle. They may be hiding somewhere in the ruins. I'll have a look here.'

The children crouched together in the cave. How they hoped that their boat would not be found! How they hoped that no one would find any traces of them at all! Timmy growled softly, wishing that he could go and find that Stinker-dog again. It had been lovely to bite his ears hard.

Edgar was half scared of finding the children, and a good deal more scared of coming up against Timmy somewhere. So he didn't make much of a search for either the children or the boat. He went into the cove where the boat had been pulled up, and although he saw traces where the vessel had been hauled up, barely smoothed out by the seawater at high tide, he didn't notice the seaweedy prow of the boat sticking out around the rock behind which it was hidden.

'Nothing here!' he called to his mother, who was looking around the ruins, peering into every likely nook. But she found nothing, and neither did Mr Stick.

'Couldn't have been the children's dog,' said Mr Stick, at last. 'They'd be here if he was, and so would their boat, but there's no sign of them at all. That dog must have been some wild stray. Have to look out for him, no doubt about it. Gone wild, I should think.'

The children relaxed after about an hour, thinking that the Sticks must have given up looking for them. They boiled the kettle to make some tea, and Anne began to cut some sandwiches. Timmy was tied up in case he wandered out again to look for Stinker.

They ate their tea quietly, not speaking above a whisper.

'The Sticks haven't come here to look for us, after all,' said Julian. 'It's obvious from what they said that they thought we had all gone to catch the train home.'

'Then what are they here for?' demanded George, fiercely. 'It's *our* island! They've no right here. Let's go and turn them off! They're scared of Timmy. We'll take him with us and say we'll set him on to them if they don't clear out.'

'No, George,' said Julian. 'Be sensible. We don't want them rushing off and telling your father we're here, or he may lose his temper and come flying home to order us back. And – there's another thing I've thought of.'

'What?' asked the others, seeing Julian's eyes gleam in the way they did when he had an idea.

'Well,' said Julian, 'don't you think it's possible that the Sticks are something to do with the smugglers? Don't you think they may come here to take off smuggled goods, or to hide them till they can take them off in safety? Mr Stick's a sailor, isn't he? He'd know all about smuggling. I bet he's in the pay of the smugglers.'

'I bet you're right!' said George, in excitement. 'Well – we'll wait till the Sticks have gone, and then we'll go down into the dungeons and see if they've hidden anything there! We'll find out their little game and stop it! It will be so exciting!'

## 16  The Sticks get a fright

But the Sticks didn't go! The children peeped out of the spy-hole at the top of the cave roof every now and again, and saw one or other of the Sticks. The evening went on and it began to be dark. Still the Sticks didn't go. Julian ran down to the nearby shore and discovered a small boat there. So the Sticks had managed to find their way around the island, rowed near the wreck, maybe landed on it too, and then come to the shore, cleverly avoiding the rocks.

'It looks as if the Sticks have come to stay for the night,' said Julian, gloomily. 'This is going to spoil our stay here, isn't it? We rush away here to escape from the Sticks – and now they're on top of us again. It's not fair.'

'Let's frighten them,' said George, her eyes shining by the light of the one candle in the cave.

'What do you mean?' said Dick, cheering up.

He always liked George's ideas, mad as they sometimes were.

'Well, I suppose they must be living down in one of the dungeon rooms, mustn't they?' said George. 'There's no place in the ruins to live in proper shelter, or we'd be there ourselves – and the only other place is down in the dungeons. I wouldn't like to sleep there myself, but I don't suppose the Sticks would mind.'

'Well, what about it?' said Dick. 'What's your idea?'

'Couldn't we creep down, and do a bit of shouting, so that the echoes start up all around?' said George. 'You know how frightening we found the echoes when we first went down into the dungeons. We only had to say one or two words, and the echoes began saying them over and over again shouting them back at us.'

'Oh yes, I remember,' said Anne. 'And wasn't Timmy frightened when he barked! The echoes barked back at him, and he thought there were thousands of dogs hiding down there! He was really frightened.'

'It's a good idea,' said Julian. 'Serve the Sticks right for coming to our island like this! If we can frighten them away, that would be one up to us! Let's do it.'

'What about Timothy?' said Anne. 'Hadn't we better leave him behind?'

'No. He can come and stand at the dungeon entrance to guard it for us,' said George. 'Then if any of the real smugglers come, Timmy can warn us. I'm not going to leave him behind.'

'Come on, then, let's go now!' said Julian. 'It would be a great trick to play. It's quite dark, but I've got my torch, and as soon as we're certain that the Sticks are down in the dungeons, we can start to play our joke.'

There was no sign or sound of the Sticks anywhere about. No light of fire or candle was to be seen, no sound of voices to be heard. Either they had gone, or they were below in the dungeons. The stones had been taken from the entrance, so the children felt sure they were down there.

'Now Timmy, you stay quite still and quiet here,' whispered George to Timmy. 'Only bark if anyone comes. We're going down into the dungeons.'

'I think I'll stay up here with Timothy,' said Anne, suddenly. She didn't like the dark look of the dungeon entrance. 'You see, George –

Timmy might be frightened or lonely up here by himself.'

The others knew Anne was frightened. Julian squeezed her arm. 'You stay here, then,' he said, kindly. 'You keep Timmy company.'

Then Julian, George and Dick went down the long flight of steps that led into the deep old dungeons of Kirrin Castle. They had been there the summer before, when they had been seeking for lost treasure; now here they were again!

They crept down the steps and came to the many cellars or dungeons cut out of the rock below the castle. There were lots of those, some big and some small, strange, damp underground rooms in which, maybe, unhappy prisoners had been kept in the olden days.

The children crept down the dark passages. Julian had a piece of white chalk with him, and drew a chalk line here and there on the rocky walls as he went, so that he could easily find the way back.

Suddenly they heard voices and saw a light. They stopped and whispered softly together in each other's ears.

'They're in that room where we found the

treasure last year! That's where they're camping out! What noises shall we make?'

'I'll be a cow,' said Dick. 'I can moo exactly like a cow. I'll be a cow.'

'I'll be a sheep,' said Julian. 'George, you be a horse. You can whinny and hrrrumph just like a horse. Dick, you start!'

So Dick began. Hidden behind a rocky pillar, he opened his mouth and mooed dolefully, like a cow in pain. At once the echoes took up the mooing, magnified it, sent it along all the underground passages, till it seemed as if a thousand cows had wandered there and were mooing together.

'Moo – oo – oo – ooooooo, ooo – oo – mooooooo!'

The Sticks listened in amazement and fright at the sudden awful noise.

'What is it, Ma?' said Edgar, almost in tears. Stinker crouched at the back of the cave, terrified.

'It's cows,' said Mr Stick, amazed. 'I think it's cows. Can't you hear the moos? But how did cows get to be here?'

'Nonsense!' said Mrs Stick, recovering herself a

little. 'Cows down these caves! You're mad! You'll be telling me there're sheep next!'

It was funny that she should have said that, for Julian chose that moment to begin baa-ing like a flock of sheep. His one long, bleating 'baa-baa-aa-aa' was taken up by the echoes at once, and it seemed suddenly as if hundreds of poor lost sheep were baa-ing their way down the dungeons!

Mr Stick jumped to his feet, as white as a sheet.

'Well, if it isn't sheep now!' he said. 'What's up? What's in these 'ere dungeons? I never did like them.'

'Baa-baa-baa-aa-AAAAAAAAAA!' went the mournful bleats all around. And then George started her whinnying and neighing, just like an impatient horse. She tossed her head in the darkness and hrrrumphed exactly like a horse and then she stamped with her foot, and at once the echoes stamped too, sending her whinnying and neighing and stamping into the Sticks's cave twenty times louder than George had made them.

Poor Stinker began to whine pitifully. He was frightened almost out of his life. He pressed himself against the floor as if he would like to disappear into it. Edgar clutched his mother's arm.

'Let's go up,' he said. 'I can't stay here. There're hundreds of sheep and horses and cows roaming these dungeons, you can hear them. They're not real, but they've got voices and hoofs, and I'm scared of them.'

Mr Stick went to the door of the room they were in, and shouted loudly.

'Get out, you! Clear out! Whoever you are!'

George giggled. Then she shouted out in a very deep, hoarse voice.

'Be-ware!' And the echoes thundered out all around.

''Ware! 'Ware! 'Ware-are-are!'

Mr Stick went back quickly into the cave room, and lit another candle. He shut the big wooden door that led into the room. His hands were shaking.

'Peculiar goings-on,' he said. 'Shan't stay here much longer if we get this kind of thing happening every night.'

Julian, Dick and George were now in such a state of giggles that they couldn't imitate any more cows, horses or sheep. George did begin to be a pig, and gave such a realistic snort and grunt that Dick nearly died of laughing. The snorts and grunts were echoed everywhere.

'Come out,' gasped Julian, at last. 'I'll burst with trying not to laugh. Come out!'

'Come out!' whispered the echoes. 'Come out, out, out!'

They stumbled out, stuffing hankies into their mouths as they went, following Julian's chalk marks easily by the light of his torch. It was impossible to take the wrong passage if they followed his guiding lines.

They sat on the dungeon steps with Anne and Timmy, and choked with laughter as they related all they had done. 'We heard old Stick yelling to us to clear out,' said George, 'and he sounded scared stiff. As for Stinker, we never heard even the smallest growl from him. I bet the Sticks will clear off tomorrow after this! It must have given them a terrible scare.'

'Oh, that was hilarious!' said Julian. 'It was a shame I started to laugh. I was just about to trumpet like an elephant. The echoes would like that!'

'Funny the Sticks all staying on the island like this,' said Dick, thoughtfully. 'They've left Kirrin Cottage – but they're not looking for us. They *must* be in league with the smugglers. Perhaps that's why Mrs Stick took the job with your mum, George – to be near the island when the time came – when the smugglers wanted their help.'

'We could go back to Kirrin Cottage, couldn't we?' said Anne, who, much as she loved the island, wasn't nearly so keen on it now that the Sticks were there.

'Go back! Leave an adventure just when it's beginning!' said George, scornfully. 'Don't be silly, Anne. Go back if you want to – but I'm sure nobody will go with you.'

'Oh, Anne will stay with us all right,' said Julian, knowing that Anne would feel hurt at the suggestion she should leave them. 'It'll be the Sticks who have to go, don't worry!'

'Let's go back to the cave,' said Anne, thinking longingly of its safety and bright little candle. They got up and made their way across the courtyard to the little wall that ran around the castle. They climbed over it and turned their steps to the cliff. Julian switched on his torch when he thought it was safe, for it was impossible to see clearly in the dark, and he didn't want any of them to fall down the hole, instead of climbing down properly by the rope.

Julian stood by the hole at last, shining his torch so that the others could climb down the rope in safety, one by one. He glanced up, looking over the dark sea as he stood there, and then stared intently.

There was a light out to sea, and it was signalling. It must have seen his torchlight! Julian watched, wondering if it was a ship that was signalling, and how far out it was, and why it was signalling.

'Perhaps they're going to put more stuff into the old wreck for the Sticks to find,' he thought. 'I wonder if they are. I'd like to find out – but it'd be dangerous to go there in daylight in case the Sticks see us.'

The signalling went on for a long time, as if a message was being flashed. Julian couldn't for the life of him make out what it was. It simply looked like the flash-flash-flash of a lantern to him. But it must be a signal or message of some sort to the Sticks.

'Well, they won't get it tonight!' thought Julian, with a chuckle, when at last the signalling stopped. 'I think the Stick family will stay where they are tonight, too scared of sheep and cows and horses rushing about in those dungeons!'

Julian was right – the Sticks did stay where they were! Nothing would get them out of their underground room till morning.

# 17  A shock for Edgar

The children slept well that night, and as Timothy didn't growl at all, they were sure that nothing important could have happened. They had a good breakfast of ham, tinned peaches, bread and butter, golden syrup and ginger beer.

'That's the end of the ginger beer, I'm afraid,' said Julian, regretfully. 'I think ginger beer is a great drink – seems to go with absolutely everything.'

'That was the nicest meal I've ever had,' said Anne. 'We do have lovely meals on Kirrin Island. I wonder if the Sticks are having nice meals too.'

'I bet they are!' said Dick. 'I expect they've ransacked Aunt Fanny's cupboards and taken the best they can find.'

'Oh, the thieves!' said George, her eyes flashing. 'I never thought of that – they may have robbed the house and taken all kinds of things.'

'They probably have,' said Julian, and he frowned. 'I never thought of that. How awful, George, if your mother came back, feeling ill and weak, and found half her belongings gone!'

'Oh dear!' said Anne, upset. 'George, wouldn't that be awful?'

'Yes,' said George, looking very angry. 'I'd believe anything of those Sticks! If they have the cheek to come to our island and live here, they've the cheek to steal from my mum's house. I wish we could find out.'

'They could have brought quite a lot of things away in their boat,' said Julian. 'They must have come here by boat. If they did bring stolen goods, they must have put them somewhere – down in the dungeons, I suppose.'

'We could have a look around and see if we can find anything, without the Sticks seeing us,' suggested Dick.

'Let's have a look around now,' said George, who always liked doing things at once. 'Anne, will you do the washing up and tidy our cave-house for us?'

Anne was torn between wanting to go with the others, and longing to play 'house' again. She loved arranging everything and making the beds and tidying up the cave. In the end she said she would stay and the others could go.

So up the rope they went. Timothy stayed with Anne, because they were afraid he might bark. Anne tied him up, and he whined a little, but didn't make a terrible noise.

The other three lay flat on the cliff-top, looking down on the ruined castle. There seemed to be no one about, but, even as they watched, the three Sticks appeared, apparently coming up from the dungeons. They seemed glad to be in the sunshine, and the children weren't surprised, for the dungeons were so cold and dark.

The Sticks looked all around. Stinker kept close to Mrs Stick, his tail well down.

'They're looking for the cows and sheep and horses they heard down in the dungeons last night!' whispered Dick to Julian.

The Sticks spoke together for a minute or two, and then went off in the direction of the shore that faced the wreck. Edgar went to the room in which the children had first planned to sleep – the one whose roof had fallen in.

'I'm going to stalk the two Sticks,' whispered

Julian to the others. 'You two see what Edgar's up to.'

Julian disappeared, keeping behind bushes as he watched where the Sticks went, and followed them. George and Dick went cautiously and quietly over the cliff to the castle in the middle of the little island. They could hear Edgar whistling. Stinker was running about the courtyard of the castle.

Edgar appeared out of the ruined room, carrying a pile of cushions, which had evidently been stored there. George went red with rage and clutched Dick's arm fiercely.

'Mum's best cushions!' she whispered. 'Oh, the thieves!'

Dick felt angry too. Obviously the Sticks had helped themselves to anything handy when they had left Kirrin Cottage. He picked up a clod of earth, took careful aim, and flung it into the air. It fell between Edgar and Stinker, breaking into a shower of earth.

Edgar dropped the cushions, and looked up into the air in fright. It was plain that he thought something had fallen from the sky. George picked up another clod, took aim, and flung it higher into the air. It fell all over Stinker, and the dog gave a yelp, and scuttled down the hole that led into the dungeons.

Edgar looked up into the sky and then all around and about him, his mouth wide open. What could be happening? Dick waited until he was looking in the opposite direction, and then once more sent a big clod into the air. It fell into bits and scattered itself all over the startled Edgar.

Then Dick gave one of his realistic moos, exactly like a cow in pain, and Edgar stood rooted to the spot, almost frightened out of his skin. Those cows again! Where were they?

Dick mooed again, and Edgar gave a yell, found his feet, and almost fell down the dungeon steps. He disappeared with a dismal howl, leaving behind all the cushions on the ground.

'Quick!' said Dick, jumping to his feet. 'He won't be back for a few minutes. He'll be too scared. Let's grab the cushions and bring them here. I don't see why the Sticks should use them down in those old dungeons.'

The two children raced to the courtyard, picked up the cushions and raced back to their hiding place. Dick looked across to the room where Edgar had brought them from.

'What about slipping across there and seeing what else they've stored away?' he said. 'I don't see why they should be allowed to have anything that isn't theirs.'

'I'll go across, and you keep watch by the dungeon entrance,' said George. 'You've only got to moo again if you see Edgar, and he'll run for miles.'

'Right,' said Dick, with a grin, and went swiftly to the flight of steps that led underground to the dungeons. There was no sign of Edgar at all, nor of Stinker.

George went to the ruined room and gazed around in anger. Yes, the Sticks certainly *had* helped themselves to her mother's things, no doubt about that! There were blankets and silver and all kinds of food. Mrs Stick must have gone into the big cupboard under the stairs and taken out various things stored there for weekly use.

George ran to Dick. 'There are heaps of our things!' she said, in a fierce whisper. 'Come and help me to get them. We'll see if we can take them all before Edgar appears, or the Sticks come back.'

Just as they were whispering together, they heard a low whistle. They looked around, and saw Julian coming along. He joined them.

'The Sticks have rowed off to the wreck,' he said. 'They've got an old boat somewhere down among those rocks. Old Pa Stick must be a good sailor to be able to take the boat in and out of those hidden rocks.'

'Oh, then we've got time to do what we want to do,' said Dick, pleased. He hurriedly told Julian about the things George had seen in the ruined room.

'Horrible thieves!' said Julian, indignantly. 'They don't mean to go back to Kirrin Cottage, that's clear. They've got some business on with the smugglers here – and when that's done they'll go off with all their stolen goods, join a ship somewhere, and get off scot-free.'

'No, they won't,' said George at once. 'We are going to get everything and take it to the cave! Dick's going to keep watch for Edgar at the cave entrance, and you and I, Julian, can quickly carry the things away. We can drop them down the hole into the cave.'

'Hurry then!' said Julian. 'We must do it before

the Sticks return, and I don't expect they'll be long. They've probably gone to fetch the trunk and anything else in the wreck. You know I saw a light out at sea last night – maybe that's a signal that the smugglers were leaving something in the wreck for the Sticks to fetch.'

George and Julian ran to the ruined room, piled their arms with the goods there, and then ran to hide them on the cliff, ready to take them to the hole when they had time. It looked as if the Sticks had just taken whatever was easiest to lay their hands on. They had even got the kitchen clock!

Edgar didn't appear at all, so Dick had nothing to do but sit by the steps of the dungeon and watch the others. After some time Julian and George gave a sigh of relief and beckoned to Dick. He left his place and went to join them.

'We've got everything now,' said Julian. 'I'm just going to the cliff-edge to see if the Sticks are returning yet. If they're not we'll all carry the things to the hole in the roof of the cave.'

He soon returned. 'I can see their boat tied to the wreck,' he said. 'We're safe for a while yet. Come on, let's get the things to safety! This is a bit of luck.'

They carried the things to the hole and called down it to Anne. 'Anne! We've got tons of things to put down the hole. Stand by to catch!'

Soon all kinds of things came down the hole into the cave! Anne was astonished. The silver and anything that might be hurt by a fall was first wrapped up in the blankets, and then let down by a rope.

'Brilliant!' said Anne. 'This cave will *really* look like a house soon, when I have arranged all these things too!'

Just as they were finishing their job the children heard voices in the distance.

'The Sticks are back!' said Julian, and looked cautiously over the cliff-top. He was right. They had returned to their boat, and were now on their way back to the castle, carrying the trunk from the wreck.

'Let's follow them, and see what happens when they find everything gone,' grinned Julian. 'Come on, everyone!'

They wriggled over the cliff on their tummies, and came to a clump of bushes behind which they could hide and watch. The Sticks put the trunk down, and looked around for Edgar. But Edgar was nowhere to be seen.

'Where's that boy?' said Mrs Stick, impatiently. 'He's had plenty of time to do everything. Edgar! Edgar! Edgar!'

Mr Stick went to the ruined room and peeped inside. He came back to Mrs Stick.

'He's taken everything down,' he said. 'He must be down in the dungeon. That room's empty.'

'I told him to come up and sit in the sun when he'd finished,' said Mrs Stick. 'It isn't healthy down in those dungeons. EDGAR!'

This time Edgar heard, and his head appeared, looking out of the entrance to the dungeon. He looked extremely scared.

'Come on up!' said Mrs Stick. 'You've got all the things down, and you'd better stay up here in the sunshine now.'

'I'm scared,' said Edgar. 'I'm not staying up here alone.'

'Why not?' said Mr Stick, astonished.

'It's those cows again!' said poor Edgar. 'Hundreds of them, Pa, all a-mooing around me, and throwing things at me. They're dangerous animals, they are, and I'm not coming up here alone!'

## 18  An unexpected prisoner

The Sticks stared at Edgar as if he was mad.

'Cows throwing things?' said Mrs Stick at last. 'What do you mean by that? Cows can't throw anything.'

'These ones did,' said Edgar, and then began to exaggerate in order to make his parents sympathise with him. 'They were dreadful cows, they were – hundreds of them, with horns as long as reindeer, and awful mooing voices. And they threw things at me and Tinker. He was really scared, and so was I. I dropped the cushions I was taking down, and rushed away to hide.'

'Where are the cushions?' said Mr Stick, looking around. 'I can't see any cushions. I suppose you'll tell us the cows ate them.'

'Didn't you take everything down into the dungeons?' demanded Mrs Stick. 'Because that room's empty now. There's not a thing in it.'

'I didn't take anything down at all,' said Edgar,

coming cautiously out of the dungeon entrance. 'I dropped the cushions just about where you're standing. What's happened to them?'

'Look 'ere!' said Mr Stick, in amazement. 'Who's been 'ere since we've been gone? Someone's taken the cushions and everything else too. Where have they put them?'

'Pa, it was the cows,' said Edgar, looking all around as if he expected to see cows walking off with cushions and silver and blankets.

'Shut up about the cows,' said Mrs Stick, suddenly losing her temper. 'For one thing there aren't any cows on this island, and that we do know, for we looked all over it this morning. What we heard last night must have been strange sort of echoes rumbling around. No – there's something funny about all this. Looks as if there *is* somebody on the island!'

A dismal howl came echoing up from below the ground. It was Stinker, terrified at being alone below, and not daring to come up.

'Poor lamb!' said Mrs Stick, who seemed much fonder of Stinker than of anyone else. 'What's up with him?'

Stinker let out an even more doleful howl, and

Mrs Stick hurried down the steps to go to him. Mr Stick followed her, and Edgar lost no time in going after them.

'Quick!' said Julian, standing up. 'Come with me, Dick. We may just have time to get that trunk! Run!'

The two boys ran quickly down to the courtyard of the ruined castle. Each took a handle of the small trunk, and lifted it between them. They staggered back to George with it.

'We'll take it to the cave,' whispered Julian. 'You stay here a few minutes and see what happens.'

The boys went over the cliff with the trunk. George flattened herself behind her bush and watched. Mr Stick appeared again in a few minutes, and looked around for the trunk. His mouth fell open in astonishment when he saw that it was gone. He yelled down the entrance to the dungeon.

'Clara! The trunk's gone!'

Mrs Stick was already on her way up, with Stinker close beside her and Edgar just behind. She climbed out and stared around.

'Gone?' she said, in enormous surprise. 'Gone!

Where's it gone?'

'That's what *I'd* like to know!' said Mr Stick. 'We leave it here a few minutes – and then it goes. Walks off by itself – just like all the other things!'

'There's someone on this island,' said Mrs Stick. 'And I'm going to find out who it is. Got your gun, Pa?'

'I have,' said Mr Stick, slapping his belt. 'You get a good stout stick too, and we'll take Tinker. If we don't ferret out whoever's trying to spoil our plans, my name's not Stick!'

George slipped away quietly to warn the others. Before she slid down the rope into the cave, she pulled several bramble sprays across the hole. She dropped down to the floor of the cave, and told the others what had happened.

Julian had been trying to open the trunk, but it was still locked. He looked up as George panted out her tale.

'We'll be all right here as long as no one falls down that hole in the roof!' he said. 'Now keep quiet everyone, and don't you dare to growl, Timmy!'

Nothing was heard for some time, and then

Stinker's bark came in the distance. 'Quiet now,' said Julian. 'They're near here.'

The Sticks were up on the cliff once more, searching carefully behind every bush. They came to the great bush behind which the children often hid, and saw the flattened grass there.

'Someone's been here,' said Mr Stick. 'I wonder if they're in the middle of this bush – it's thick enough to hide half an army! I'll try and force my way in, Clara, while you stand by with my gun.'

Edgar wandered off by himself while this was happening, feeling certain that nobody would be foolish enough to live in the middle of such a prickly bush. He walked across the cliff – and then, to his awful horror, he found himself falling! His legs disappeared into a hole, he clutched at some thorny sprays but couldn't save himself. Down he went and down and down – and down – crash!

Edgar had fallen down the hole in the roof of the cave. He suddenly appeared before the children's startled eyes, and landed in a heap on the soft sand. Timmy at once pounced on him with a fearsome growl, but George pulled him off just in time.

Edgar was half-stunned with fright and his fall. He lay on the floor of the cave, groaning, his eyes shut. The children stared at him and then at one another. For a few moments they were completely taken aback and didn't know what to do or say. Timmy growled ferociously – so ferociously that Edgar opened his eyes in fright. He stared around at the four children and their dog in the utmost surprise and horror.

He opened his mouth to yell for help, but at once found Julian's large hand over it.

'Yell just once and Timmy will have a bite out of any part of you he likes!' said Julian, in a voice as ferocious as Timothy's growl. 'Like to try it? Timmy's waiting to bite.'

'I won't yell,' said Edgar, speaking in such a low whisper that the others could hardly hear him. 'Keep that dog off. I won't yell.'

George spoke to Timothy. 'Now you listen, Timothy – if this boy shouts, you just go for him! Lie here by him and show him your big teeth. Bite him wherever you like if he yells.'

'Woof!' said Timmy, looking really pleased. He lay down by Edgar, and the boy tried to move away. But Timmy came nearer every time he moved.

Edgar looked around at the children. 'What are you doing on this island?' he said. 'We thought you'd gone home.'

'It's *our* island!' said George, in a very fierce voice. 'We've every right to be on it if we want to – but you have no right at all. None! What are you and your dad and mum here for?'

'Don't know,' said Edgar, looking sulky.

'You'd better tell us,' said Julian. 'We know you're in league with smugglers.'

Edgar looked startled. 'Smugglers?' he said. 'I didn't know that. Pa and Ma don't tell me anything. I don't want anything to do with smugglers.'

'Don't you know *any*thing?' said Dick. 'Don't you know why you've come to Kirrin Island?'

'I don't know anything,' said Edgar, in an injured tone. 'Pa and Ma are mean to me. They never tell me anything. I do as I'm told, that's all. I don't know anything about smugglers, I tell you that.'

It was obvious to the children that Edgar really didn't know anything of the reasons for his parents coming to the island.

'Well, I'm not surprised they don't let Spotty-Face into their secrets,' said Julian. 'He'd blab them if he could, I bet. Anyway, we know it's smuggling they're mixed up in.'

'You let me go,' said Edgar, sullenly. 'You've got no right to keep me here.'

'We're not going to let you go,' said George at once. 'You're our prisoner now. If we let you go back to your parents, you'd tell them all about us, and we don't want them to know we're here. We're going to spoil their little plans, you see.'

Edgar saw. He saw quite a lot of things. He felt rather sick. 'Was it you that took the cushions and things?'

'Oh no, Edgar,' said Dick. 'It was the cows, wasn't it? Don't you remember how you told your mum about the hundreds of cows that mooed at you and threw things and stole the cushions you dropped? Surely you haven't forgotten your cows already?'

'Funny, aren't you?' said Edgar, sulkily. 'What you going to do with me? I won't stay here, that's flat.'

'But you will, Spotty-Face,' said Julian. 'You'll stay here till we let you go – and that won't be till we've cleared up this little smuggling mystery. And let me warn you that any nonsense on your part will be punished by Timmy.'

'Lot of bullies you are,' said Edgar, seeing that he could do nothing but obey the four children. 'My pa and ma won't half be furious with you.'

His ma and pa were feeling extremely astonished. There had, of course, been nobody hiding in the big thick bush, and when Mr Stick had wriggled out, scratched and bleeding, he had looked around for Edgar. And Edgar wasn't to be seen.

'Where's that dratted boy?' he said, and shouted for him. 'Edgar! Ed-gar!'

But Edgar didn't answer. The Sticks spent a very long time looking for Edgar, both above ground and underground. Mrs Stick was convinced that poor Edgar was lost in the dungeons, and she tried to send Stinker to find him. But Stinker only went as far as the first cave. He remembered the peculiar noises of the night before and wasn't at all keen on exploring the dungeons.

Julian turned his attention to the little trunk, once Edgar had been dealt with. 'I'm going to open this somehow,' he said. 'I'm sure it's got smuggled goods in.'

'You'll have to smash the locks then,' said Dick.

Julian got a small rock and tried to smash the two locks. He managed to wrench one open after a while, and then the other gave way too. The children threw back the lid.

On the top was a child's blanket, embroidered with white rabbits. Julian pulled it off, expecting to see the smuggled goods below. But to his astonishment there were a child's clothes!

He pulled them out. There were two blue jumpers, a blue skirt, some vests and knickers and a warm coat. At the bottom of the trunk were some dolls and a teddy bear!

'How strange!' said Julian, in amazement. 'What are all these for? Why did the Sticks bring these to the island – and why did the smugglers hide them in the wreck? It's a mystery!'

Edgar appeared to be as astonished as the rest. He too had expected valuable goods of some kind. George and Anne pulled out the dolls. They were lovely ones. Anne admired them. She liked dolls, though George hated them.

'Who do they belong to?' Anne said. 'Won't they be sad not to have them! Julian, isn't it funny? *Why* should anyone bring a trunk full of clothes and dolls to Kirrin Island?'

## 19 A scream in the night

Nobody could even guess the answers to Anne's surprised questions. The children stared into the trunk and puzzled over it. It seemed such a funny thing to smuggle. They remembered the other things in the wreck too – the tins of food. They were peculiar things to smuggle on to the island. There didn't seem any point in it.

'Funny,' said Dick, at last. 'It beats me. There's no doubt that strange things are going on here, or the Sticks wouldn't be hanging around our island. And we've seen signals from a ship out to sea. Something's going on. We thought if we opened this trunk it might help us – but it's only made the mystery deeper.'

Just then the voices of the two parent Sticks could be heard shouting for Edgar. But Edgar didn't dare to shout back. Timmy's nose was poked against his leg. He might be nipped at any time. Timmy growled every now and again to remind Edgar that he was still there.

'Do you know anything about the ship that signals to this island at night?' asked Julian, turning to Edgar.

The boy shook his head. 'Never heard of any signals,' he said. 'I just heard my ma saying that she expected the *Roamer* tonight, but I don't know what she meant.'

'The *Roamer*?' said George, at once. 'What's that – a man – or a boat – or what?'

'I don't know,' said Edgar. 'I'd only have been told off if I'd asked. Find out yourself.'

'We will,' said Julian, grimly. 'We'll watch out for the *Roamer* tonight! Thanks for the information.'

The children spent a quiet and rather boring day in the cave – all except Anne, who had plenty of things to arrange again. The cave looked really home-like when she had finished! She put the blankets on the bed, and used the rugs as carpets. The cave really looked very impressive!

Edgar wasn't allowed to go out of the cave, and Timothy didn't leave him for a moment. He slept most of the time, complaining that 'those cows and things' had frightened him so much the night before that he'd not been able to sleep a wink.

The others discussed their plans in low voices. They decided to keep watch on the cliff-top, two and two together, that night. They would wait and see what happened. If the *Roamer* came, they would hurriedly make fresh plans then.

The sun sank. The night came up dark over the sea. Edgar snored softly, after a very good supper of sardines, corned-beef sandwiches, tinned apricots and tinned milk. Anne and Dick went up to keep the first watch. It was about half-past ten.

At half-past twelve Julian and George climbed up the knotted rope and joined the other two. They had nothing to report. They went down into the cave, got into their comfortable beds and went to sleep. Edgar was snoring away in his corner, Timmy still on guard.

Julian and George looked out to sea, watching for any sign of a ship. The moon was up that night, and things weren't quite so dark. Suddenly they heard low voices, and saw shadowy figures down by the rocks below.

'The two Sticks,' whispered Julian. 'Going to row out to the wreck again, I suppose.'

There was the splash of oars, and the children saw a boat move out over the water. At the same time George nudged Julian violently and pointed out to sea. A light was being shown a good way out, from a ship that the children could barely see. Then the moon went behind a cloud, and they could see nothing for some time.

They watched breathlessly. Was that shadowy ship the *Roamer*? Or was the owner of it the *Roamer*? Were the smugglers at work tonight?

'There's another boat coming – look!' said George. 'It must be coming from that ship out at sea. Now the moon has come out again, you can just see it. It's going to the old wreck. It must be a meeting place, I should think.'

Then, most irritatingly, the moon went behind a cloud again, and remained there so long that the children grew impatient. At last it sailed out again and lit up the water.

'Both boats are leaving the wreck now,' said Julian excitedly. 'They've had their meeting – and passed over the smuggled goods, I suppose – and now one boat is returning to the ship, and the other, the Sticks's boat, is coming back here with the goods. We'll follow the Sticks when they get back and see where they put the goods.'

After a long time the Sticks's boat came to shore again. The children couldn't see anything then, but at last they saw the Sticks going back towards the castle. Mr Stick carried what looked like a large bundle, flung over his shoulder. They couldn't see if Mrs Stick carried anything.

The Sticks went into the courtyard of the castle, and came to the dungeon entrance.

'They're taking the smuggled goods down there,' whispered Julian to George. The children were now watching from behind a nearby wall. 'We'll go back and tell the others, and make some more plans. We must somehow or other get those goods ourselves, and take them back to the mainland and get in touch with the police!'

Just then a scream rang out in the night. It was a high-pitched, terrified scream, and frightened the watching children very much. They had no idea where it came from.

'Quick! It must be Anne!' said Julian, and the two ran as fast as they could to the hole that led down to the cave. They dropped down the rope and Julian looked around the quiet cave anxiously. What had happened to Anne to make her scream like that?

But Anne was peacefully asleep on her bed, and so was Dick. Edgar still snored and Timmy watched, his eyes gleaming green.

'Funny,' said Julian, still startled. 'Really funny. Who screamed like that? It couldn't possibly have been Anne – because if she had screamed in her sleep like that, she would have woken the others.'

'Well, who screamed, then?' said George, feeling rather scared. 'Wasn't it strange, Julian? I didn't like it. It was somebody who was really frightened. But who could it be?'

They woke Dick and Anne and told them about the strange scream. Anne was very startled. Dick was interested to hear that two boats had met at the wreck, and that the Sticks had brought back smuggled goods of some sort, and taken them down in the dungeons.

'We'll get those tomorrow, somehow!' he said, cheerfully. 'We'll have good fun.'

'Why did you think it was me screaming?' asked Anne. 'Did you think it was a girl screaming?'

'Yes. It sounded like the scream you give when one of us jumps out at you suddenly,' said Julian.

'It's funny,' said Anne. She cuddled down into her bed again, and George got in beside her.

'Oh Anne!' said George, in disgust. 'You've got our bed *full* of those dolls – and that teddy bear is here too! You're such a baby!'

'No, I'm not,' said Anne. 'The dolls and the bear are frightened and lonely because they're not with the little girl they belong to. So I had them in bed with me instead! I'm sure the little girl would be glad.'

'The little girl!' said Julian, slowly. 'We thought we heard a little girl scream tonight – we found a small trunk full of a little girl's clothes, and a little girl's dolls. What does it all mean?'

There was a silence – and then Anne spoke excitedly. 'I know! The smuggled goods are a little girl! They've stolen a little girl away – and these are her dolls, and those over there are her clothes that were stolen at the same time, for her to dress in and play with. The little girl's here, on this island now – you heard her scream tonight when those horrible Sticks carried her down into the dungeons!'

'I think Anne has hit on the right idea,' said Julian. 'You clever thing, Anne! I think you're right. It isn't smugglers who are using this island – it's kidnappers!'

'What are kidnappers?' said Anne.

'People who steal away children or grown-ups and hide them somewhere till a large sum of money is paid out for them,' explained Julian. 'It's called a ransom. Till the ransom is paid, the prisoner is held by the captors.'

'Well, that's what's happened here then!' said George.

'I bet it has! Some poor little rich girl has been stolen away – and brought to the wreck by boat from some ship – and taken over by those horrible Sticks. Wicked creatures!'

'And we heard the poor little thing scream just as she was taken down underground,' said George. 'Julian, we've got to rescue her.'

'Yes, of course,' said Julian. 'We will! We'll rescue her tomorrow.'

Edgar woke up and joined in the conversation suddenly. 'What you talking about?' he said. 'Rescue who?'

'Never you mind,' said Julian.

George nudged him and whispered.

'All I hope is that Mrs Stick is feeling as upset

about losing her dear Edgar as the mother of the little girl,' she said.

'Tomorrow we find the little girl somehow, and take her away,' said Julian. 'I expect the Sticks will be on guard, but we'll find a way.'

'I'm tired now,' said George, lying down. 'Let's go to sleep. We'll wake up nice and fresh. Anne, please put these dolls on your side. I'm lying on at least three.'

Anne took the dolls and the bear and arranged them on her side of the bed. Soon they were all asleep – all except Timothy, who lay with one eye open all night long. There was no need to put anyone on guard while Timmy was there. He was the best guardian they could have.

## 20  A rescue – and a new prisoner!

The next day Julian was awake early and went up the rope to the cliff-top to see if the Sticks were about. He saw them coming up the steps that led from the dungeons. Mrs Stick looked pale and worried.

'We've got to find our Edgar,' she kept saying to Mr Stick. 'I tell you we've got to find our Edgar. He's not down in the dungeons. That I do know. We've yelled ourselves hoarse down there.'

'And he's not on the island,' said Mr Stick. 'We hunted all over it yesterday. I think whoever was here took our goods, caught Edgar, and made off with him and everything else in their boat. That's what I think.'

'Well, they've taken him to the mainland then,' said Mrs Stick. 'We'd better take our boat and go back there and ask a few questions. What I'd like to know is – who is it messing about here and interfering with our plans? It makes me scared.

Just when things are going nicely too!'

'Is it all right to leave here just now?' said Mr Stick, doubtfully. 'Suppose whoever was here yesterday is still here – they might pop down into the dungeons when we're gone.'

'Well, they're not here,' said Mrs Stick, firmly. 'Use your common sense, if you've got any – wouldn't our Edgar yell the place down if he was being kept prisoner on this little island – and wouldn't we hear him? I tell you he must have been taken off in a boat, together with all the other things that are gone. And I don't like it.'

'All right, all right!' said Mr Stick, in a grumbling tone. 'That boy's always a nuisance – always in silly trouble of some sort.'

'How can you talk of poor Edgar like that?' cried Mrs Stick. 'Do you think the poor child *likes* being captured? Goodness knows what he's going through – feeling frightened and lonely without me.'

Julian felt disgusted. Here was Mrs Stick talking like that about old Spotty-Face – and yet she had a little girl down in the dungeons – a child much younger than Edgar! What a nasty woman she was.

'What about Tinker?' said Mr Stick, in a sulky tone. 'Better leave him here, hadn't we, to guard the entrance to the dungeons? Not that there will be anyone here, if what you say is right.'

'Oh, we'll leave Tinker,' said Mrs Stick, setting off to the boat.

Julian saw them go, leaving the dog behind. Tinker watched them rowing away, his tail well down between his legs. Then he turned and ran back to the courtyard, and lay down dolefully in the sun. He was very uneasy. His ears were cocked and he kept looking this way and that. He didn't like this strange island and its unexpected noises.

Julian tore back to the cave and dropped down the rope, startling Edgar very much.

'Come outside the cave and I'll tell you my plans,' said Julian to the others. He didn't want Edgar to hear them.

They all went outside. Anne had got breakfast ready while Julian had been gone, and the kettle was boiling away on the little stove.

'Listen!' said Julian. 'The Sticks have gone off in their boat back to the mainland to see if they can find their precious Edgar. Mrs Stick is all hot and bothered because she thinks someone's gone off with him and she's afraid the poor boy will be feeling frightened and lonely!'

'*Well!*' said George. 'Doesn't she think that the little kidnapped girl must be feeling much worse? What a horrible woman she is!'

'You're right,' said Julian. 'Well, what I think we should do is this – we'll go down into the dungeons now and rescue the little girl – and bring her here to our cave for breakfast. Then we'll take her off in our boat, go to the police, find out where her parents are, and phone to let them know that she's safe.'

'What shall we do with Edgar?' said Anne.

'I know!' said George at once. 'We'll put Edgar into the dungeon instead of the little girl! Think how surprised the Sticks will be to find the little girl gone and their dear Edgar shut up in the dungeon instead!'

'Oooh! – that *is* a good idea,' said Anne, and all the others laughed and agreed.

'You stay here, Anne, and cut some more bread and butter for the little girl,' said Julian. He knew that Anne hated going down into the dungeons.

Anne nodded, pleased.

'All right, I will. I'll just take the kettle off for a

bit too, or else the water will boil away.'

'They all went back into the cave. 'Come with us, Edgar,' said Julian. 'You come too, Timmy.'

'Where're you going to take me?' said Edgar, suspiciously.

'A nice cosy, comfortable place, where cows can't get at you,' said Julian. 'Come on! Hurry up.'

'Gr-r-r-r-r,' said Timmy, his nose against Edgar's leg. Edgar got up in a hurry.

They all went up the rope one after another, though Edgar was scared, and was sure he couldn't. But with Timmy snapping at his ankles below, he climbed up the rope remarkably quickly, and was hauled out at the top by Julian.

'Now, quick march!' said Julian, who wanted to get everything over before the Sticks thought of returning. And quick march it was, over the cliffs, over the low wall of the castle, and down into the courtyard.

'I'm not going down into those dungeons with you,' said Edgar, in alarm.

'You are, Spotty-Face,' said Julian, amiably.

'Where's my Pa and Ma?' said Edgar, looking anxiously all around.

'Those cows have got them, I expect,' said

George. 'The ones that came and mooed at you and threw things, you know.'

Everyone giggled, except Edgar, who looked worried and pale. He didn't like this kind of adventure at all. The children came to the dungeon entrance, and found that the Sticks had not only closed down the stone that opened the way to the dungeons, but had also dragged heavy rocks across it.

'Bother your parents!' said Julian, to Edgar. 'Making a lot of trouble for everybody. Come on, stir yourself – all hands to these stones. Edgar, pull when we pull. Go on! You'll get into trouble if you don't.'

Edgar pulled with the rest, and one by one the rocks were moved away. Then the heavy trapdoor stone was hauled up too, and the flight of steps was exposed leading down into darkness.

'There's Tinker!' suddenly cried Edgar, pointing to a bush some distance away. Tinker was there, hiding, quite terrified at seeing Timothy again.

'Fat lot of good Stinker is,' said Julian. 'No, Timmy – you're not to eat him. Stay here! He wouldn't taste nice if you did eat him!'

Timothy was sorry not to be able to chase

Stinker round and round the island. If he couldn't chase rabbits, he might at least be allowed to chase Stinker!

They all went down into the dungeons. Julian's white chalk marks were still on the rocky walls, so it was easy to find the way to the cave-like room where the children, last summer, had found piles of golden ingots. They felt sure that the kidnapped girl had been put there, for this cave had a big wooden door that could be bolted on the outside.

They came to the door. It was well and truly bolted. There was no sound from inside. Everyone halted outside and Timmy scratched at the door, whining gently. He knew there was someone inside.

'Hello!' shouted Julian, in a loud and cheerful voice. 'Are you all right? We've come to rescue you.'

There was a scrambling noise, as if someone had got up from a stool. Then a small voice sounded from the cave.

'Hello! Who are you? Oh, please rescue me! I'm so scared!'

'Just undoing the door!' called back Julian,

cheerfully. 'We're all children out here, so don't be afraid. You'll soon be safe.'

He shot back the bolts, and flung open the door. Inside the cave, which was lit by a lantern, stood a small girl, with a scared little white face, and large dark eyes. Dark red hair tumbled around her cheeks, and she had evidently been crying, for her face was dirty and tear-stained.

Dick went to her and put his arm around her. 'Everything's all right now,' he said. 'You're safe. We'll take you back to your mum.'

'I really want her,' said the little girl, and tears ran down her cheeks again. 'Why am I here? I don't like being here.'

'Oh, it's just an adventure you've had,' said Julian. 'It's over now – at least, nearly over. There's still a bit of it left – a nice bit, though. We want you to come and have breakfast with us in our cave. We've a lovely cave.'

'Oh, have you?' said the little girl, rubbing her eyes. 'I want to go with you, I like you, but I didn't like those other people.'

'Of course you didn't,' said George. 'Look! This is Timothy, our dog. He wants to be friends with you.'

'What a lovely dog!' said the little girl, and flung her arms around Timmy's neck. He licked her in delight. George was pleased. She put her arm around the little girl.

'What's your name?' she said.

'Jennifer Mary Armstrong,' said the little girl. 'What's yours?'

'George,' said George, and the little girl nodded, thinking that George was a boy, not a girl, for she was dressed in jeans just like Julian and Dick, and her hair was short, too, though very curly.

The others told her their names – and then she looked at Edgar, who had said nothing.

'This is Spotty-Face,' said Julian. 'He isn't a friend of ours. It was his parents who put you here, Jennifer. Now we are going to leave him here in your place. It will be such a pleasant surprise for them, won't it?'

Edgar gave a yell of dismay and tried to back away – but Julian gave him a strong shove that sent him flying into the cave.

'There's only one way to teach people like you and your parents that wickedness doesn't pay!' said the boy, grimly. 'And that's to punish you.

People like you don't understand kindness. You think it's just being soft and silly. Fine – you can have a taste of what Jennifer has had. It'll do you good, and do your parents a lot of good too! Goodbye!'

Edgar began to howl dismally as Julian bolted the big wooden door top and bottom. 'I'll starve!' he wailed.

'Oh no, you won't,' said Julian. 'There's plenty of food and water in there, so help yourself. It would do you good to go hungry for a while, all the same.'

'Mind the cows don't get you!' called Dick, and he gave a realistic moo that startled Jennifer very much, for the echoes came mooing around too.

'It's all right – only the echoes,' said George, smiling at her in the torchlight. Edgar howled away in the cave, sobbing like a baby.

'Little coward, isn't he?' said Julian. 'Come on – let's get back. I'm really hungry for my breakfast.'

'So am I,' said Jennifer, slipping her small hand into Julian's. 'I wasn't hungry at all in that cave – but now I am. Thank you for rescuing me.'

'Don't mention it,' said Julian, grinning at her.

'It's a real pleasure – and an even greater one to put old Spotty-Face there instead of you. Nice to give the Sticks a taste of their own medicine.'

Jennifer didn't know what he meant, but the others did, and they chuckled. They made their way back through the dark, musty passages of the dungeons, passing many caves, big and small, on the way. They came at last to the flight of steps and went up them into the dazzling sunlight.

'Oh!' said Jennifer, breathing in great gulps of the fresh, sea-smelling air. 'Oh! This is lovely! Where am I?'

'On our island,' said George. 'And this is our ruined castle. You were brought here last night in a boat. We heard you scream, and that's how we guessed you were being made a prisoner.'

They walked to the cliff, and Jennifer was amazed at the way they disappeared down the knotted rope. She was eager to try too, and soon slid down into the cave.

'Nice kid, isn't she?' said Julian to George. 'She's had even more of an adventure than we have!'

## 21 A visit to the police station

Anne liked Jennifer very much, and gave her a hug and a kiss. Jennifer looked around the well-furnished cave in amazement and wonder – and then she gave a scream of surprise and joy. She pointed to Anne's neatly made bed, on which sat a number of beautiful dolls, and a large teddy bear.

'My dolls!' she said. 'Oh, and Teddy, too! Where did you get them? Josephine and Angela and Rosebud and Marigold, have you missed me?'

She flung herself on the dolls. Anne was very interested to hear their names. 'I've looked after them well,' she told Jennifer. 'They're quite all right.'

'Thank you,' said the little girl, happily. 'I do think you're all nice. Oh, what a lovely breakfast!'

It was. Anne had opened a tin of salmon, two tins of peaches, a tin of milk, cut some bread and butter, and made a big jug of cocoa. Jennifer sat down and began to eat. She was very hungry, and as she ate, she began to lose her paleness and look rosy and happy.

The children talked busily as they ate. Jennifer told them about herself.

'I was playing in the garden with my nanny,' she said, 'and suddenly, when she had gone indoors to fetch something, a man climbed over the wall, threw a shawl around my head, and took me away. We live by the sea, and I heard the sound of the waves splashing on the shore, so I knew I was being put into a boat. I was taken to a big ship, and locked down in a cabin for two days. Then I suppose I was brought here one night. I was so frightened that I screamed.'

'That was the scream we heard,' said George. 'It was lucky we heard it. We had thought there was smuggling going on here, on our island – we didn't guess it was a case of kidnapping, till we heard you scream – though we had found your trunk with your clothes and toys.'

'I don't know how the man got those,' said Jennifer. 'Maybe one of our servants helped him. There was one I didn't like. She was called Sarah Stick.'

'Ah!' said Julian, at once. 'That's the one, then! It was Mr and Mrs Stick who brought you here. Sarah Stick must be a relation of theirs. They must have been in the pay of someone else, I expect – someone who had a ship, and could bring you here to hide you.'

'It's a good hiding place,' said George. 'No one but us would ever have found it out.'

They ate all their breakfast, made some more cocoa, and discussed their plans.

'We'll take our boat and go to the mainland this morning,' said Julian. 'We'll go straight to the police station with Jennifer. I expect the newspapers are full of her disappearance, and the police will recognise her at once.'

'I hope they catch the Sticks,' said George. 'I hope they won't disappear into thin air as soon as they hear that Jennifer is found.'

'Yes – we must warn the police of that,' said Julian, thoughtfully. 'Better not spread the news till the Sticks are caught. I wonder where they are?'

'Let's get the boat now,' said Dick. 'There's no point in waiting. Jennifer's parents will be so relieved to know she's safe.'

'I don't want to leave this lovely cave,' said Jennifer, who was thoroughly enjoying herself now. 'I wish I lived here, too. Are you going to come back to the island and live here, Julian?'

'We'll come back for a few days more, I expect,' said Julian. 'Our aunt's home is empty at the moment because she's away ill and our uncle is with her. So we might as well stay on our island till they come back.'

'Oh, *could* I come back with you?' begged Jennifer, her small round face alight with joy at the thought of living in a cave on an island with these nice children and their lovely dog. 'Oh, please let me! I'd really like it. And I love Timmy.'

'I don't expect your parents would let you, especially after you've just been kidnapped,' said Julian. 'But you can ask them, if you like.'

They all went to the boat and got in. Julian pushed off. George steered the boat in and out of the rocks. They saw the wreck, which interested Jenny very much indeed. She badly wanted to stop, but the others thought they ought to get to land as quickly as possible.

Soon they were near the beach. Alf, the

fisherman's son was there. He saw them and waved. He ran to help them to pull in their boat.

'I was coming out in my boat this morning,' he said. 'Your dad's back, George. But not your mum. She's getting better, they say, and will be back in a week's time.'

'Well, what's my dad come back for?' demanded George, in surprise.

'He got worried because nobody answered the telephone,' explained Alf. 'He came down and asked me where you all were. I didn't tell him, of course. I kept your secret. But I was just coming out to warn you this morning. He got back last night – and he was so angry! No one there to give him any food – all the house upside down and half the things gone! He's at the police station now.'

'That's where *we*'re going too!' said George. 'We'll meet him there. Oh dear, I hope he won't be in a temper. You can't do anything with Dad when he's cross.'

'Come on!' said Julian. 'It's a good thing, in a way, that your father is here, George – we can explain everything to him and to the police at the same time.'

They left Alf, who looked very surprised to see Jennifer with the others. He couldn't make out where she had come from. She hadn't started out to the island with them – but she had come back in their boat. How had that happened? It seemed very mysterious to Alf.

The children arrived at the police station and marched in, much to the surprise of the policeman there.

'Hello!' he said. 'What's the matter? Been doing a burglary, or something, and come to own up?'

'Listen!' said George, suddenly, hearing a loud voice in the room next to theirs. 'That's Dad's voice!'

She darted to the door. The policeman called to her, shocked.

'Now don't you go in there. The Inspector's in there. Come over here special, he has, and mustn't be interrupted.'

But George had flung open the door and gone inside. Her father turned and saw her. He rose to his feet. 'George! Where have you been? How dare you go away like this and leave the house and everything! It's been robbed! I've just been telling the Inspector about all the things that have been stolen.'

'Don't worry, Dad,' said George. 'Really don't worry. We've found them all. How's Mum?'

'Better, much better,' said her father, still looking amazed and angry. 'Thank goodness I can go back and tell her where you are. She kept asking me about you all, and I had to keep saying you were all right, so as not to worry her – but I hadn't any idea what was happening to you or where you had gone. I'm very cross with you. Where were you?'

'On the island,' said George, looking rather sulky, as she often did when her father was angry with her. 'Julian will tell you all about it.'

Julian came in, followed by Dick, Anne, Jennifer and Timothy. The Inspector, a big, clever-looking man with dark eyes under shaggy eyebrows, looked at them all closely. When he saw Jennifer, he stared hard – and then suddenly rose to his feet.

'What's your name, little girl?' he said.

'Jennifer Mary Armstrong,' said Jenny, in a surprised voice.

'I can't believe it!' said the Inspector, in a

startled voice. 'Here's the child the whole country is looking for – and she walks in here as cool as a cucumber! Where did she come from?'

'What do you mean?' said George's father, looking surprised. 'What child is the whole country looking for? I haven't read the papers for some days.'

'Then you don't know about little Jenny Armstrong being kidnapped?' said the Inspector, sitting down and pulling Jenny near him. 'She's the daughter of Harry Armstrong, the millionaire. Well, somebody kidnapped her and wants a hundred thousand pounds ransom for her. We've combed the country for her – and here she is! Well, this is the strangest thing I ever knew. Where have you been, young lady?'

'On the island,' said Jenny. 'Julian – you tell it all.'

So Julian told the whole story from beginning to end. The policeman from outside came in, and took notes down as he spoke. Everyone listened in amazement. As for George's father, his eyes nearly fell out of his head. What adventures these children had, and how well they managed everything!

'And do you happen to know who was the owner of the ship that brought Jenny along – the one that sent a boat off to the wreck and put her there for the Sticks to take?' asked the Inspector.

'No,' said Julian. 'All we heard was that the *Roamer* was coming that night.'

'Aha!' said the Inspector, with great satisfaction in his voice. 'We know the *Roamer* all right – a ship we've been watching for some time – owned by somebody we're very, very suspicious of – we think he's dabbling in a whole lot of shady deals. Now this is very good news indeed. The thing is – where are the Sticks – and how can we catch them red-handed, now you've got Jenny out of their clutches? They'll probably deny everything.'

'I know how we could catch them,' said Julian quickly. 'We've left their nasty son, Edgar, locked in the same dungeon where they put Jenny. If one of us could tell the Sticks, that that's where Edgar is, they'd go back to the island, and go right into the dungeons If you found them there, it wouldn't be much good them denying that they don't know anything about the island, and have never been there.'

'That would certainly make things a lot easier,' said the Inspector. He pressed a bell and another policeman came into the room. The Inspector gave him a full description of Mr and Mrs Stick, and told him to search the area for them, and report when they were found.

'Then, Julian, you might like to go and have a little conversation with them about their son, Edgar,' said the Inspector, smiling. 'If they do go back to the island, we'll follow them, and get all the evidence we want. Thank you for your very great help. Now we must phone Jenny's parents and tell them she's safe.'

'She can come back to Kirrin Cottage with us,' said George's father, still looking rather dazed at all that had happened. 'I've got Joanna, our old cook, to come back for a while to put things straight, so there will be someone there to see to the children. They must all come back.'

'Well, Dad,' said George, firmly, 'we'll come back just for today, but we plan to spend another week on Kirrin Island till Mum comes back. She said we could, and we're having such a good time there. Let Joanna stay at Kirrin Cottage and keep it in order and get it ready for Mum when she comes home – she won't want the bother of looking after us too. We can look after ourselves on the island.'

'I certainly think these children deserve a reward for the good work they have done,' remarked the Inspector, and that settled the matter.

'Very well,' said George's father, 'you can all go off to the island again – but you must be back when your mother returns, George.'

'Of course I will,' said George. 'I really want to see Mum. But home isn't nice without her. I'd rather be on our island.'

'And I want to be there, too,' said Jenny, unexpectedly. 'Ask my parents to come to Kirrin, please – so that I can ask them if I can go with the others.'

'I'll do my best,' said the Inspector, grinning at the five children. They liked him very much. George's father stood up.

'Come along!' he said. 'I want my lunch. All this has made me feel hungry. We'll go and see if Joanna has got anything for us.'

Off they all went, talking nineteen to the dozen, making George's poor father feel completely bewildered. He always seemed to get into the middle of some adventure when these children were about!

## 22  Back to Kirrin Island!

Soon everyone was at Kirrin Cottage. Joanna, the cook they had had before, gave them a good welcome, and listened to their adventures in astonishment while getting the lunch ready.

It was while they were having lunch that Julian, looking out of the window, suddenly caught sight of a figure he knew very well – someone skulking along behind the hedge.

'Old Pa Stick!' he said, and jumped up. 'I'll go after him. Stay here, everyone.'

He went out of the house, ran around a corner and came face to face with Mr Stick.

'Do you want to know where Edgar is?' said Julian mysteriously.

Mr Stick looked startled. He stared at Julian not knowing what to say.

'He's down in the dungeons, locked in that cave,' said Julian, even more mysteriously.

'You don't know anything about Edgar,' said

Mr Stick. 'Where have you been? Didn't you go home?'

'Never you mind,' said Julian. 'But if you want to find Edgar – look in that cave!'

Mr Stick gave the boy a glare and left him. Julian hurried indoors and rang the police station. He felt sure that Mr Stick would tell Mrs Stick what he had said, and that Mrs Stick would insist on going back to the island to see if what he had said was true. So all that needed to be done was for the police to keep a watch on the boats along the shore and see when the Sticks left.

The children finished their dinner, and Uncle Quentin announced that he must return to his wife, who would want to know his news. 'I'll tell her you're having a good time on the island,' he said, 'and we can tell her all the extraordinary details when she comes home, better.'

He left in his car, and the children wondered whether to return to their island. But they decided to wait a little, for they didn't know what to do with Jennifer.

Very soon a large car drove up and stopped outside the gate of Kirrin Cottage. Out jumped a tall man with dark red hair, and a pretty woman.

'They must be your father and mother, Jenny,' said Julian.

They were – and Jennifer got so many hugs and kisses that she almost lost her breath. She had to tell her story again and again, and her father couldn't thank Julian and the others enough for all they had done.

'Ask me for any reward you like,' he said, 'and you can have it. I'll never, never be able to tell you how grateful I am to you for rescuing our little Jenny.'

'Oh – we don't want anything, thank you,' said Julian, politely. 'We enjoyed it all very much. We like adventures.'

'But you *must* tell me something you want!' said Jenny's father.

Julian glanced around at the others. He knew that none of them wanted a reward. Jenny nudged him hard and nodded her head vigorously. Julian laughed.

'Well,' he said, 'there *is* one thing we'd all like very much.'

'It's granted before you ask it!' said Jenny's father.

'Will you let Jenny come and spend a week

with us on our island?' said Julian. Jenny gave a squeal and pressed Julian's arm very hard between her two small hands.

Jenny's parents looked rather taken aback.

'Well,' said her father, 'she's just been kidnapped – and we don't really want to let her out of our sight at the moment – and . . .'

'You promised Julian you'd grant what he asked, you promised, Dad,' said Jenny, urgently. 'Oh please let me. I've always wanted to live on an island. And this one has got an amazing cave, and a wonderful ruined castle, and the dungeons where I was kept, and—'

'And we take Timothy, our dog, with us,' said Julian. 'See how big he is – nobody could come to much harm with Timmy about – could they, Tim?'

'Woof!' said Timothy, in his deepest voice.

'Well, you can go, Jenny, on one condition,' said the little girl's father at last, 'and that is that your mother and I come over tomorrow and spend the day on the island, to see that everything is all right for you.'

'Oh, thank you, thank you, Dad!' cried Jenny, and danced around the room in delight. A whole week on the island with these new friends of hers, and Timmy the dog! What could be lovelier?

'Jenny can stay here the night, can't she?' said George. 'You'll be staying at the hotel, I suppose?'

Soon Jenny's parents left and went to the police station to get all the details of the kidnapping. The children went to see if Joanna was going to make cakes for tea.

At tea-time there was a knock at the door. A large policeman stood outside.

'Is Julian here?' he said. 'Oh, you're the boy we want. The Sticks have just left for the island in their boat, and we've got ours on the beach to follow. But we don't think we know the way in and out of those hidden rocks that lie all around Kirrin Island. Could you or Georgina guide us, do you think?'

'I'm George, not Georgina,' said George in a cold voice.

'Sorry,' said the policeman, with a grin. 'Well, could you come too?'

'We'll all come!' said Dick, jumping up. 'I want to go back to the island and sleep in our cave again tonight. Why should we miss a single night?

We can fetch Jenny's parents tomorrow in our own boat. We'll all come.'

The policeman was a little doubtful about the arrangement, but the children insisted, and as there was no time to waste, they all ended up crowding into the two boats, with three big policemen, George and Julian leading the way in their own boat. Timmy lay down at George's feet as usual.

George guided the boat as cleverly as ever, and soon they landed in the usual little sandy cove. The Sticks had evidently gone around by the wreck as usual, and landed on the rockier part.

'Now, no noise,' said Julian, warningly. They all went quietly towards the ruin, and came into the courtyard. There was no sign of the Sticks.

'We'll go down underground,' said Julian. 'I've got my torch. I expect the Sticks are down there already, letting out Edgar.'

They went down the steps into the dark dungeons.

Anne went too, this time, holding the hand of one of the big policemen. They moved quietly through the long, dark, winding passages.

They came at last to the door of the cave in

which they had imprisoned Edgar. It was still bolted at the top and bottom!

'Look!' said Julian, in a whisper, shining his torch on to the door. 'The Sticks haven't been down here yet.'

'Shh!' said George, as Timmy growled softly. 'There's someone coming. Hide! It's the Sticks, I expect.'

They all hid behind the wall that ran nearby. They could hear footsteps coming nearer, and then the voice of Mrs Stick raised in anger.

'If my Edgar's locked in there, I'll have something to say about it! Locking up a poor innocent boy like that. I don't understand it. If he's there, where's the girl? You answer me that. Where's the girl? I think the boss has done some double-crossing to do us out of our share of the money. Didn't he say that he'd give us two thousand pounds if we kept Jenny Armstrong for a week? He must have sent someone to this island, played tricks on us, taken the girl himself and locked up our Edgar.'

'You may be right, Clara,' said Mr Stick, his voice coming nearer and nearer. 'But how did this boy Julian know where Edgar was? There's a lot

I don't understand about all this.'

Now the Sticks were right at the door of the cave, with Stinker at their heels. Stinker smelt the others in hiding and whined in fear. Mr Stick kicked him.

'Stop it! It's enough to hear our own voices echoing all around without your whines too!'

Mrs Stick was calling out loudly: 'Edgar! Are you there? Edgar!'

'Ma! Yes, I'm here!' yelled Edgar. 'Let me out, quick! I'm scared. Let me out!'

Mrs Stick undid the bolts at once and flung open the door. By the light of the lantern in the cave she saw Edgar. He ran to her, half crying.

'Who put you here?' demanded Mrs Stick. 'You tell your Pa and he'll knock their heads off, won't you, Pa? Putting a poor frightened child into a dark cave like this. It's a wicked thing to do!'

Suddenly the Stick family had the fright of their lives – for a large policeman stepped out of the shadows, torch in one hand and notebook in the other!

'You're right, Clara Stick,' said the policeman, in a deep voice. 'To shut up a poor frightened child in that cave *is* a wicked thing to do – and that's what you did, isn't it? You put Jenny Armstrong there! She's only a little girl. This boy of yours knew he wasn't coming to any harm – but that little girl was scared to death!'

Mrs Stick stood there, opening and shutting her mouth like a goldfish, not finding a word to say. Mr Stick squealed like a rat caught in a corner.

'We're caught! It's a trap, that's it. We're caught!'

Edgar began to cry, sobbing like a four-year-old. The other children felt disgusted with him. The Sticks suddenly caught sight of all the children when Julian switched on his torch.

'Look! There's all the children – and there's Jenny Armstrong too!' said Mr Stick, in a tone of the greatest amazement. 'What's all this? What's happening? Who shut up Edgar?'

'We'll tell you the answers when we get to the police station,' said the big policeman. 'Now, are you coming quietly?'

The Sticks went quietly, Edgar sobbing away to himself. He imagined his mother and father in prison, and he himself sent to a hard and difficult school, not allowed to see his mother for years. He didn't understand that his parents were no good to him, and had taught him nothing but bad things. There might be a chance for the boy if he were kept away from them, and set a good example instead of a bad one.

'We won't be coming back with you,' said Julian, politely, to the policeman. 'We're staying here the night. You could go back in the Sticks's boat. They know the way. Take their dog with you. There he is – Stinker, we call him.' Then he added, 'I guess your colleagues could follow in the police boat!'

The Sticks's boat was found and the policeman, the two grown-up Sticks and Edgar got in. Stinker jumped in too, glad to get away from the glare of Timothy's green eyes.

Julian pushed the boat out. 'Goodbye!' he called, and the other children waved goodbye, too. 'Goodbye, Mr Stick, don't go kidnapping any more children. Goodbye, Mrs Stick, look after Edgar better, in case *he* gets kidnapped again! Goodbye, Spotty-Face, try to be a better boy! Goodbye, Stinker, get a bath as soon as possible. Goodbye!'

The policemen grinned and waved. The Sticks said not a word, nor did they wave. They sat sullen and angry, trying to work out what had happened to make things end up like this.

The boats rounded a high rock and were soon out of sight.

'Hurray!' said Dick. 'They've gone – gone forever! We've got our island to ourselves at last. Come on, Jenny, we'll show you all over it! What a fun time we're going to have.'

They raced away, happy and carefree, five children and a dog, alone on an island they loved. And we will leave them there to enjoy their week's happiness. They really do deserve it!

# Enid Blyton

# THE
# FAMOUS FIVE'S
# SURVIVAL GUIDE

*Packed with useful information on surviving outdoors and solving mysteries, here is the one mystery that the Famous Five never managed to solve. See if you can follow the trail to discover the location of the priceless Royal Dragon of Siam.*

*The perfect book for all fans of mystery, adventure and the Famous Five!*

ISBN 9780340970836

Meet Peter, Janet and Jack, Barbara, Pam, Colin and George. Together they are The Secret Seven — ready to solve any mystery, anytime!
A great introduction to adventure stories.